His smile was dangerous. Jade had the sensation that she was in deep trouble now.

His melting eyes contemplated her mouth. 'I know. We could play guessing games.'

'Guess . . .' Her voice tailed away into thin air.

'Yes, you shut your eyes and guess where I'm going to touch you next and if you get it wrong, I kiss you.'

'What . . . ?' Jade cleared her choked throat. She was going to regret asking this. 'What if I get it right?' she breathed.

'Oh, then I kiss you, of course,' he smiled.

Her brain seemed focused on the way his fingers were exploring the contours of her naked back. 'I don't want to play any games. I want . . .'

'Me,' he growled throatily.

'Dane . . .'

'Sweet Jade, you can't carry a torch for your late husband for ever,' he said gently. 'You are young and beautiful and in need of loving. Here I am, here you are—you can't stay faithful to his memory all your life. I'm here, real, alive and needing you . . . Let me help you forget him.'

Forget! If only she could!

TENDER PERSUASION

BY

SARA WOOD

MILLS & BOON LIMITED
ETON HOUSE 18-24 PARADISE ROAD
RICHMOND SURREY TW9 1SR

First published in Great Britain 1988 by Mills & Boon Limited

© Sara Wood 1988

Australian copyright 1988 Philippine copyright 1988 This edition 1988

ISBN 0 263 76143 6

Set in Plantin 10 on 11½ pt. 01 – 8811 – 54024

Typeset in Great Britain by JCL Graphics, Bristol

Made and printed in Great Britain

CHAPTER ONE

'INCREDIBLE! It balances!' marvelled Jade, looking at the school-dinner book in amazement.

The man sitting opposite her in the cramped, untidy office grinned at her relief. 'Cracked it at last, have you?' he asked.

'It was all the dinners uneaten by children who were at home ill that foxed me. And the grubby little envelopes with coins missing didn't help.' She began to bag up the money, to take to the post office.

'It's not really your kind of environment here, is it?' observed John Pavey, leaning forward on his desk. 'I am grateful to you for helping out this term, Jade.'

She smiled at him. It had been her salvation, losing herself in the intricacies of orders for mundane things like exercise books and paintbrushes. There was the added bonus, too—the fun of being a teacher's helper.

'You're doing me a favour as well, don't forget that.' Her long lashes swept down on her cheekbones as she surveyed herself critically. 'Am I really such a round peg in a square hole?'

John chuckled. 'Let's say you're the most unorthodox school secretary I've ever worked with. Don't get me wrong, though, I look forward to your mornings here with enormous and gleeful anticipation.'

'Because you never know what's going to happen?' she asked wryly.

'Absolutely,' he enthused. 'Apart from me, I've noticed

the children turning up earlier and earlier as well. They love it when you do your stints in the classroom.'

'I love it, too,' she laughed, her teeth glistening white in her dark-skinned face. Jade had inherited her mother's Italian colouring—and her temperament. 'I don't think I'll forget our day at the manor in a hurry.'

'Heaven, pure heaven,' grinned John. 'Especially when little Billy Love fell into the pond and discovered he could swim, and you had to go in to get him eventually, because he wouldn't come out!'

'Glad someone enjoyed my unscheduled dip! Oh, darn,' she cried, hearing the church clock striking. 'I've taken so long that the post office will be shut by the time I get there.' She began to gather up the money bags, and searched for her shoes under the desk.

'Knock on the cottage door. Mrs Love will let you in, especially as Billy worships the water you swim in.'

Jade laughed as she slipped her feet into the battered sandals. 'I doubt that she was very keen on washing out the duckweed and mud from his clothes,' she said. 'Bye, then, see you tomorrow.'

'What will the morrow bring?' murmured John to himself. 'More to the point, what will you bring?'

'Wait and see,' she said darkly, waggling her black brows in a sinister fashion.

She left the chuckling John, hoisted up her long cotton skirts and hurtled along the winding village street.

John heard her frantic dash and smiled in amusement. Life was always one mad whirl with Jade around. The village was still reeling from the shock.

Saxonbury lay in the ancient Hundred of Holmestrowe, a group of early Saxon settlements running across the valley of the River Ouse in Sussex. Its lands stretched from the high downland to the river and marshland, and up to the downs on the other side of the valley. Each village had been laid out in the same way to provide a fair share of the land resources. Saxonbury people could graze sheep and cattle on the downs and use the rich meadows in the valley for cutting hay. Above the flood plain and close to the village was the ploughland, and from the air, when the evening sun slanted its rays, the old feudal strip system of fields could still be seen.

The flint and brick village school dated from 1856. With John as its head, it was comprised of two classrooms: the fourteen infants in one and seventeen juniors in another. There was one full-time teacher of the little ones, and a part-timer who shared duties with John Pavey. It was a close-knit community, and when the school secretary fell ill with glandular fever John was loath to use a supply from County Hall in Lewes.

He knew that Jade Kendall needed taking out of herself after her recent troubles. She could type, and not only did she produce the Church newsletter each week, but she had written several children's books which were in the school library. When she came to interview him about the history of the school for her book on Saxonbury itself, he plucked up courage and asked if she would fill the temporary vacancy.

Jade had only been working there for a week, but already the place had come alive because of her. He hadn't known her very well since she came to live in the manor house two years ago—in fact the villagers had disliked her smooth husband, Sebastian, and disapproved of the parties and goings-on.

But since young Sebastian Kendall's sudden death, Jade had not entertained and was often seen walking the fields with her golden retriever. The villagers found her solitary grief and quiet life admirable, and warmed to her. Now, of course, Jade had other problems on her plate.

John sighed and returned to writing the week's events in the school log-book. A lot to put in for a change! Yet . . . for all Jade's exuberance and sheer joy of living, he'd sensed loneliness and pain behind those lovely brown eyes. The next few months would be terrible for her: he wouldn't change places with her for all the world.

Jade skidded to a halt at Deep Thatch, her long black hair flying in all directions and her shoulder-bag banging on her slender hip. This was Mrs Love's small cottage and, on Monday and Friday mornings, it was also the village post office. As she'd thought, it was closed. Then she noticed that her big shoulder-bag had flopped open and two of the money bags hadn't been properly pushed down inside it, nor had they been thoroughly sealed!

Her slim body whirled around in dismay, sending the fashionably shaggy mane of glossy hair whipping over her face. She pushed it back irritably. There were shiny coins dotted over the tarmac. How many had she lost? She tried not to think of the old adage 'more haste, less speed', and sat down on the grassy verge to count the contents of the two unsealed bags, emptying each one in a separate pile on to the soft gold and yellow of her patterned skirt.

'Fifteen, sixteen . . . oh, bother!'

She'd lost concentration at the sound of a throaty car revving around the twisting lane that led from the main road. A tourist. They often came down to investigate the small village with its quaint old cottages and the decaying manor, or called in to see the birthplace of the famous writer, Barlock Weir.

'One, two . . .' Jade didn't look up as the car turned the

bend because she was determined to count the money and find what she could before making up the difference. Money was one of her problems nowadays, and the reason for the posters which had just gone up, announcing that the manor was for sale.

Thinking of this, she miscounted again and looked up crossly to see an incredibly ostentatious and sleek black sports car pulling to a halt a few inches away.

Maserati, six cylinder, she registered, her eyes reflecting pain. Sebastian had owned one once.

'Afternoon,' came a rich velvet voice.

Jade tore her eyes from the gleaming bodywork of the car and focused on its occupant. He was examining her openly, with the kind of thoroughness that men reserved for race-horses! Offended by his scrutiny of her face, even more offended by his close interest in her body and resenting the way his dark eyes became sensuous when they reached her full breasts in the thin top, she decided to reciprocate in kind.

Her highly arched mouth, untouched by lipstick, curved into a slight sneer. The man was a smoothie. She hated and despised smoothies. His hair, a little dishevelled from the open sports car, was nevertheless neatly cut, the black line where it met his tanned neck being immaculate, and only the few curls flopping on the broad forehead disturbed the impression of a well-groomed head.

That was because his features were perfect, she mused. Skin a Miami bronze, as smooth and unblemished as satin and glowing with health. Probably worked out every morning in a London gym, judging by the width of the shoulders and that chest. He must be a City man: no one else would drive around these parts in such a flamboyant car, nor would they wear a black pinstripe with a pastel yellow shirt and matching hanky and rose in the middle of May!

Critically she examined his hands. Terribly well manicured—the man obviously had never done a day's real work in his life. And they reminded . . .

'I wonder if you could help me?' he murmured.

'I haven't finished staring, yet,' she said sweetly.

He chuckled. '*Touché*. Shall I get out? You can't appreciate all of me like this. Far too much is hidden from your view.'

Jade was startled. Ogling men were usually disconcerted by her directness; they weren't supposed to co-operate!

'I've seen enough, thank you. I——'

Too late, he was easing himself over the door, his long legs and strong arms managing the vault without difficulty. Perhaps he was expecting her to clap in admiration, she thought scornfully. He was definitely a gym fanatic.

'That better?' He leant casually against the car, his thighs indecently close to Jade's face.

'You're crowding me.' She glared, then turned her attention to the money. One, two, three . . .

'Your worldly wealth?' he asked, squatting down.

'Bother! I've lost count again!' she muttered.

'Allow me.' His hand dipped intimately into her lap, scooping up one pile of coins, and Jade recoiled at his temerity, her mouth tightening as he flicked her a smiling glance and wickedly raised an eyebrow. In seconds, however, he had checked the money in his hand and she watched grimly while he totted up the rest. 'Four pounds twenty in that lot and two pounds seventy-eight here,' he declared.

'Darn!'

'You need a bit more? Saving up for a black cat?'

Jade's angry brown eyes met his deep blue ones. 'A cat?' she repeated stupidly.

'When I saw you, sitting by the roadside with your skirt spread out enticingly and layers of frothy white petticoat showing, I thought: aha, the village enchantress,' he grinned, his eyes melting into hers. 'The river of black hair did nothing to disprove my theory. And then I saw your slanting eyes and enchanting mouth and knew you were casting a spell on me.'

'Don't be ridiculous,' she mumbled, quite flustered by his approach. How dared he try to pick her up?

'This place feels as if it has stood still for the last hundred years,' he murmured. 'And finding a woman like you,' his eyes made a quick appraisal of her from top to toe, 'turning over coins by the wayside——'

'I've lost the dinner money,' she snapped, deciding to put an end to the man's outrageous flirting. Now the money was back in its bags, she could get up safely. But he'd risen with her, and stood smiling down in a very smug and self-satisfied way. 'Move aside, I've got to find it.'

It was the stranger's turn to look puzzled. 'Dinner money? You have to save up to eat?'

Despite herself, Jade couldn't help grinning at the idea. Pushing him aside, she began to pick up coins on the road.

'My goodness,' said a voice in her ear. 'This is fun. Your streets are paved with ten-pence pieces.'

Jade chuckled, the dimple in her cheek dancing. 'They fell out of the bags as I ran,' she said.

'And why were you running, and where were you going, and will you tell me what's going on before I burst with curiosity?' he demanded, finding money faster than she could.

Jade's head reeled at the quickfire delivery, and knew

for the first time what it was like to be on the receiving end
of her own breathless speeches.

'This is the dinner money paid by the children in the
village school,' she explained, reaching out for a coin and
finding her fingers grasping his. He shot her a look, half
amused, half sensual, and she snatched her hand away in
irritation. Wretched flirt!

'And you were running off with it,' he said, jumping into
the ditch and bringing back some coins. 'You planned to
leave the country and buy a villa in Marbella.'

Jade noticed that his glove-soft black shoes had become
muddied from the tiny brook that ran through the ditch,
and smiled in satisfaction. That would teach him to tease
and pursue her!

'I was taking it to the post office. I'm the school
secretary,' she said primly.

He sat down in the the middle of the lane in astonishment, surprising Jade with the action. She would have bet
that he was a fastidious man, not given to Bohemian
behaviour. And yet he'd been unperturbed at finding his
shoes were squelching around in the ditch.

'Now that,' he said, staring hard, 'is the most bizarre
thing you've said since we met. Pull the other one.' He
stretched out his elegantly clad leg to her in offering.

With difficulty, Jade bit back a smile. He was terribly
handsome, terribly appealing and distinctly individual. She
checked his left hand and a deep sense of disappointment
welled up within her. He was also married!

Her scornful gaze swept over him and his eyebrow rose in
unspoken query. Jade tilted up her small chin and forced
herself to disregard his charm. He was making her feel
young and carefree again; she hadn't felt like that for years.
And he was entirely the wrong kind of man to be producing

those feelings!

'It's true,' she said stiffly. 'That's why I have to find every penny.' In a more frantic manner, she continued to search and was relieved to find that it was only necessary to add a little of her own money.

When she walked back, she found that he was still sitting in the middle of the road, and had been watching her all the time as she crawled along the lane on her hands and knees, presenting a good view of her rear and probably a fair amount of petticoat. Jade didn't care. She marched past him grimly, lifted the latch on Deep Thatch gate and strode rapidly up the narrow brick path.

At the old plank door, she hesitated. John had said it would be all right to knock, but she didn't like to do so.

'Are you reciting a spell for walking through doors?' called the stranger. 'Can I watch?'

'This is the post office,.' she said crossly, seeing him leaning on the gate. 'And it's closed.'

His eyes ran over the steep thatched roof which almost reached the ground on each side. Jade was grudgingly pleased that his face softened at the cottage's simple charm. He carefully examined the flint walls, almost hidden by the drooping pale blue blooms of the old wistaria which dropped its petals on the sills of the lattice windows.

A slow, broad grin changed his appearance even more. Somewhere under that slick Don Juan exterior was a man who appreciated the quality of life, thought Jade hazily.

'It's the most customer-friendly post office I've ever seen,' he said, walking up the path towards her, trying to take in every bit of the colourful cottage garden as he did so. Disconcerted by the way she found herself liking the man, she banged on the horseshoe knocker.

'Hello, Miss.' Billy had answered the door and was

displaying his gappy teeth to her.

'Hello, Billy. Drowned in any ponds lately?' she twinkled.

'I never drowned,' he objected. 'I swam. Fun, wasn't it?'

'Hilarious. I'm still finding fish and water-beetles in my hair.'

'Fancy!' Billy's eyes widened as he contemplated her thick tresses, obviously half expecting to see a golden carp gasping there.

'Um . . .' Jade saw that the man had taken up a position against the small laburnum tree and was laughing at the exchange. 'I'm awfully late, I know, but I've brought the dinner money and . . .'

'Sure. It's OK. Mum! Come in,' invited Billy. 'She's doing scones. I'll get her.'

Jade went into the small sitting-room and sat down on the chintz sofa, to find herself sharing it with the stranger.

'This isn't a free show for your benefit, you know,' she said tartly, as he folded his arms and seemed to be waiting for her to do something interesting.

'Oh! Sorry, my mistake. I thought you laid on entertainment like this for every visitor,' he said. 'Village life and all its eccentricities. Meet the locals, learn ditch crawling, spot the post office. That kind of thing.'

A treacherous giggle escaped from her lips and was fiercely suppressed.

'Don't patronise,' she said calmly. 'What do you want here, anyway? The post office is closed to anyone but me.'

'I want to ask you some questions,' he said, unconcerned. 'I'm doing a survey for the Max Planck Foundation and . . .'

'It was an Institution last time I heard,' she said drily, trying not to laugh when his face fell.

'Curses! Trust me to choose a well-read woman,' he sighed.

Inwardly, Jade sighed too. He was fun, she thought wistfully. Then she frowned. He probably had a lot of fun with his wife and family, and judging by his slick line in chat, with any willing women who fell for his disarming style.

'Hello, Jade.' Mrs Love bustled in, wiping her hands on her apron. 'Wait a minute while I open up.'

'I'm awfully sorry to be a nuisance,' she said, rising. 'I couldn't get the darn books to balance, and then I dropped some of the money . . .'

'And I picked some of it up,' came a deep voice.

'Well, now, that's nice.' Mrs Love beamed at him in evident admiration, hardly able to take her eyes from his engaging neon grin as she let down the counter from its latch on the wall. 'I always open up for late school money,' she said. 'You don't want to leave it on the premises. Let's be having it, then.'

Feeling ridiculously self-conscious, Jade carefully unpacked all the money bags and watched Mrs Love checking them with enviable speed.

'Got any more goats?'

She turned with relief to Billy, hovering in the doorway and eating home-made chocolate cake. 'No! I'm still paying for the damage the last one did!' she grinned. 'I've had to swap her with the farmer for chicken feed and a honey extractor.'

'Enlighten me,' murmured the man. 'About the goat.'

'She brought it to school,' mumbled Billy, his mouth full. 'Ate Miss Jones's basket, it did, and had a go at *French for Beginners.*'

'That's a text book,' explained Jade hurriedly. Then she remembered. 'Billy, I saw you were learning about hexagons today, so I thought you'd all like to see the bees and have a honeycomb for the nature table.'

'Oh, boy! Will they sting Miss Jones?' asked Billy hopefully.

'Monster,' chided Jade. 'My bees are well trained.'

'Better trained than the goat, I hope,' muttered a voice behind her.

Jade wished he'd keep out of their conversation. 'Haven't you got a wife to go home to?' she said pointedly.

'I have business here,' he said quietly.

Her heart lurched. Business? He couldn't be visiting the school. No schools inspector had ever been that well groomed. He . . . She refused to contemplate the possibility that flashed into her head. With an effort, she concentrated on Mrs Love's neat writing and was relieved to be signing the slip. Now she could go and forget clever City men.

'Come to see the manor, have you?' asked Mrs Love.

Oh, God! trembled Jade, as he took what seemed like interminable seconds to answer.

'That's right.'

She swallowed to rid herself of the awful dry and empty feeling in her throat. She'd known that one day she'd have to face up to showing people around, but this was too soon, she wasn't ready. In any case, he was the last person she'd sell it to! She couldn't possibly live next door to anyone like him, and know that he was carrying on a life-style similar to Sebastian's. Except for being more amusing, he was so like Sebastian's friends. His arrogance stood out a mile, even to the extent of having the nerve to turn up without an appointment. Well, he wasn't getting the guided tour today. It would give her great satisfaction to refer him to the estate agent to set up a meeting—and even greater satisfaction to stall him as long as possible.

'I thought so,' continued the post mistress. 'When I

saw you with Jade, I thought, ah, she's going to show him around.'

Mrs Love was about to say more, and Jade frantically interrupted, saying the first thing that came into her head. Anything, even showing this glib sophisticate her house, was better than having her private affairs discussed, or strangers knowing that she was the current owner. There would be too many questions, too much prying: painful answers.

'Yes,' she said hurriedly, looking at her watch. 'And we'd better hurry. Goodbye, Mrs Love, and thanks. Come on,' she called to the astonished man, still sitting on the sofa, 'we have a lot to look at.'

He jumped up with alacrity and followed her out. Jade had stumbled blindly for a few yards down the lane by the time he caught up and stopped her with a hand on her shoulder.

'Leave me alone. Let's get this over with,' she muttered, twisting away.

'No. Hold on.' He moved swiftly in front of her, his face serious. 'Who——'

'My name is Jade and I'm the school secretary, I told you,' she said, forestalling him. Surreptitiously she pushed her left hand into her pocket and slid off her wedding ring, noticing that his eyes went straight to that hand when she brought it out again. He must know that it was a Mrs Kendall who was Saxonbury Manor's current owner—or rather the owner of the second crippling mortgage. She hoped, therefore, that he had an image in his mind of a middle-aged county lady. If that was so, then he wouldn't connect Mrs Kendall with a casually dressed scatterbrain who worked in the local school. That should put him off the scent. 'I'm to show people around. The owner doesn't like the idea of selling,' she added truthfully. She wanted to sell, but dreaded the process of doing so.

'I'm sure,' he said, walking along with her again. 'It must be sad, leaving happy memories behind. I understand the husband died in some accident.'

A year ago, and still the memory cut her like a knife! 'Yes,' she said tightly, her tone discouraging further prying. He wasn't easily put off.

'What kind of accident?' he asked.

'Ballooning.' To hide her shaken expression, Jade reached up and buried her face in the deep purple lilac that hung over the lane.

'I think I remember something in the papers,' he said, frowning in concentration. 'Wasn't he trying to cross the Alps?'

'Pyrenees.'

'I'm sorry,' he said, hearing the quiver in her voice. 'I suppose in such a small community the death of one of its members must have upset the rest of the village, too. And I'm forgetting my manners. I'm Dane King.'

She took his hand reluctantly. 'I . . . That is . . . No one told me you were coming. You're only supposed to see the house by appointment,' she said, suddenly remembering she could get out of the chore and put off the evil day when a stranger first started nosing around her home.

'Oh? My secretary sent a letter a few days ago, advising that I'd be here today unless I heard to the contrary.'

Jade bit her lip, knowing what had happened.

'I'm afraid your letter was probably eaten,' she sighed.

He didn't bat an eyelid. 'I see. That would explain why Mrs Kendall didn't know I was coming,' he said as if letters were frequently devoured in his experience.

Jade dimpled, reckoning he was owed an explanation, and then paused. She must remember he didn't know who she really was.

'My goat escaped—she often did. The manor door was open and she ate the post before it could be collected.'

'I hope she wasn't ill,' he said suavely.

Her eyes slanted up at him. Either he was very good at hiding his surprise and remaining urbane, or so much had happened to him that nothing surprised him any more.

'It had almost a fatal result. I considered turning her into mince.'

'Minced goat is a delicacy I haven't tried,' he grinned. 'Did Mrs Kendall mind?'

'She was livid,' said Jade truthfully.

'I'm sure she was. She probably has a lot on her mind at the moment.'

'She has,' sighed Jade, suddenly brightening as an idea occurred to her. 'Would you like to see around the rest of the village? It might give you a feel of the place.'

He smiled down at her, unsuspecting. 'That would be wonderful,' he said huskily. 'I think feel is so important, don't you?'

She stared hard. 'You'll feel a distinct frost if you make any more stupid remarks like that,' she said coldly.

He grinned, unperturbed. 'Can't blame me for trying, can you?'

She did. Married men shouldn't roam . 'Get this straight,' she seethed. 'I'm showing you the village and then, if you want to proceed, the house. I'm not showing you anything else. I don't like smarmy City slickers, especially ones who think that life in the sticks is picturesque and romantic, and that the dawn chorus is something to do with the sound of six-cylinder engines revving up for the morning crawl to the Treasury.'

'Ouch!' he winced. 'And I thought a little peasant girl might be bowled over by my sophisticated technique,' he joked.

Her dark brown eyes looked him up and down scathingly. 'The local farm lads have a better technique than yours, and it's more successful.'

'Ah. Spoken for, are you?' he murmured.

'Over here,' she said sharply, ignoring him, 'is Barlock Weir's house. Twice a week, the village is nose to tail in worshippers of his prose style. Coaches have a standing arrangement to park in the driveway of Saxonbury Manor,' she said, exaggerating hugely. 'The new owner would be expected to honour that, of course. I hope you won't upset the villagers and ruin the joy of his admirers by changing the arrangement if you buy the house.'

She was pleased to see he was frowning as he studied the clapperboard cottage, preserved inside and out in 1920s style as it had been left when the great author died.

'That's the footpath to the school,' she continued relentlessly, 'but we won't go there now. It'll be mayhem. Playtime. Usually the harassed headmaster brings the children into the manor grounds so they can let off a bit of steam, because the playground is so tiny.' Her fingers were crossed at the small white lies she was telling. Well, John was sometimes harassed, and they did go into the manor and the playground was small. It was the way she put it together that was misleading.

'Hence Billy falling into the pond,' he said.

'Yes. Would loads of children pretending to be Superman or the Lower Sixth at St Trinian's bother you?' she asked innocently.

'Saint . . .'

'The awful girls' school, where the girls run wild and . . .'

'I know what you meant,' he said faintly. 'Yes, it would bother me. I need the house to be peaceful.'

'Oh, dear,' she said sorrowfully, looking at her feet and willing her mouth not to twitch in delight. 'The country isn't quiet, Mr King. Not here, anyway. I live next door to the manor and my cockerels are always crowing, day and night it seems. Then the tractors drone away all day and the farm machines, the forester's chainsaw . . . We're used to it, but a townie . . .'

'I could put up with a lot of things if you lived next door,' he said. 'Will you show me your house?'

Jade could have kicked herself. Since Sebastian's death, Saxonbury Manor had held too many memories for her to stay. She'd found herself thinking of the past and not planning for the future. So she had chosen to live in what was once the gardener's cottage and fought to keep the big house going, calling in every day to feed the fantails in the huge medieval dovecote, until a time when the new owner would take the burden of responsibility from her shoulders.

'You wouldn't be interested in my cottage. It's like the rest of the houses in the village,' she said in an offhand manner. 'Dark, damp and plagued with rats.'

'Sounds positively feudal,' he murmured, his thoughtful gaze on her.

She shrugged her slender shoulders and had to save her narrow strap from slipping down her arm and revealing too much flesh. Dane's avid eyes lingered on her breasts and, conscious of his interest, she tried not to walk with her usual hip-swinging motion. She had become very aware of her own sexuality and wanted to minimise it.

'We'll go into the church,' she said, opening the lych-gate. That would keep his mind on sober things, she thought crossly, wondering why the atmosphere between them was becoming tense.

'This is beautiful.' He was admiring the circular Norman

tower, one of only three in the whole of Sussex.

That wouldn't do! 'Decaying,' she said laconically. 'The whole thing is falling down. The parish council has agreed a levy from every householder to repair it. That's one of the reasons Mrs Kendall is selling up—the upkeep of the village is horrendous.'

'Surely that's not how things are done——' he began.

'Come inside,' she said quickly, almost dragging him in. 'See those roof timbers! Death-watch beetle. If you're quiet, you can hear them, clicking away. Huge beams like that are going to cost a fortune.'

She craned her neck up and tilted her head in an attitude of listening. There was a silence. Gradually she became aware that Dane King wasn't joining her in the study of non-existent death-watch beetles, but had folded his arms and was staring at her instead. As she dropped her gaze, she saw that his expression had ceased to be charming or flirtatious and was hard. And his eyes were more piercing and blazing angry than any she had ever seen.

Jade gulped. 'S-s-something wrong?' she said, to unfreeze the deathly silence.

A deep breath expanded the big chest and she gulped again, awed and intimidated by him. He was terribly angry. Had he rumbled her? Still he remained silent. Then, as she slicked her dry lips, he was seemingly galvanised into action and, before she knew what had hit her, he had caught her up and marched her outside, down the path and out on to the lane.

'Well now, Jade. It seemed inappropriate to yell at you inside a church,' he said in a soft voice that held evidence of barely controlled rage. 'So you'll explain here.'

Jade lifted her defiant eyes to his. She wasn't going to let him push her around. 'I thought I was explaining everything rather well,' she bluffed.

She gave an outraged gasp as his big hand splayed on her middle, and she staggered back till she felt her spine being pressed against the yew tree. His hand stayed where it was, pushing imperceptibly, and Jade's pride refused to allow her to prise it away.

'Why don't you want me to buy Saxonbury?' he asked grimly.

Jade's face grew serious, and she looked at him from under her thick lashes. She'd have to give him a reason of some sort.

'This is a nice village. Nice people live in it. Unwordly people. You wouldn't fit in.'

'Not enough.'

'It's all I have to say,' she said doggedly.

'Really?'

To her dismay, he moved close, his body trapping hers, his hands snaking out to catch her wrists as she moved to thrust at his shoulders. And they were body to body; her soft warmth transferring to his muscled hardness, his face harshly thrust into hers, a snarl marring the handsome features.

'I'll scream——'

'Do that and I'll kiss you,' he threatened in a biting tone.

Jade's eyes grew huge and she clamped her lips together, not daring to open them for any reason in case he interpreted that as the preliminary to a scream. The last thing she wanted was for him to kiss her! Already the shocking pressure of his body was causing some highly undesirable responses within her. It was shaming that she was responding to the highly potent virility of the kind of man she loathed.

The air was thick with an electrifying charge that ran

between them, welding them closer, rendering Jade immobile. Small tremors ran through her, till every nerve-ending felt alive and stretched to its limits. What had happened to her? Had she been corrupted morally during her marriage, without realising it?

His anger was dying away, to be replaced by another emotion far more dangerous. Their intimate situation was having its effect on him, too, as it would on any red-blooded man. He, Jade realised with a flash of fear, was more red-blooded than most.

'Well, Jade, why don't you scream?' he murmured in a sultry voice.

Unable to speak, not daring to, she shook her head in mute refusal.

'Pity. Let's pretend, then,' he said huskily, and bent to claim her mouth.

CHAPTER TWO

JADE'S whirling brain and aroused senses temporarily eclipsed the knowledge that Dane was a stranger and married. All she knew was that her instincts had completely taken over her mind and were urging her to respond to his incredibly erotic kisses. Still holding her wrists, so that their arms were outstretched, Dane shifted his body suggestively against hers, shocking Jade with his intimacy. And his desire.

She tried to twist her head away, moaning under his warm, searching, searing mouth, but he anticipated every move and his kiss deepened, setting up a terrible yearning inside her. It was because of Sebastian, of course, she thought miserably. The way he'd made love to her . . .

Tears welled into her brown eyes and she squeezed them tightly, but too late to prevent two huge, salty drops running down her face. Dane's tongue found one as he explored the arch of her upper lip.

'I don't usually make women cry when I kiss them,' he said quietly, drawing back to look at her.

'I bet you don't,' she said savagely, angry with her weakness. Her head tossed, making black tendrils flip angrily into the air. 'Now, if you've finished, perhaps you'd take your disgusting body away from mine and release my wrists.' She felt terribly vulnerable, with her breasts stretched high against his chest, and deeply ashamed that their hardened centres were throbbing in apparent abandon.

He did as she asked, and stood awkwardly while she made a show of rubbing her reddened wrists and tucking in her top more securely.

'God, I'm sorry,' he said, passing a shaking hand through his black hair.

'I should think you ought to be! I could claim assault,' she muttered.

'I know. I—I don't know what happened. One minute I wanted to throttle you and the next . . .' He shrugged. 'It was partly your fault, getting me so annoyed. I might not have touched you otherwise. You lied to me. You spun me tales about how awful it was here.'

It was Jade's turn to be discomfited. 'I think we're quits,' she said slowly.

'I wish I understood you,' said Dane, perplexed.

'They all say that,' she sighed.

'Who?'

'Oh, everyone,' she said vaguely. Few people other than her parents' crowd had experienced the odd life-style she considered to be normal. She'd despaired of ever finding anyone on her wave-length: it had been obvious that she must be the one to adapt, that she was the one out of step. This she had done, though lately she'd been living her own life in her own way. Perhaps that was why Dane King disturbed her so much: despite the fact that she was wary of him, there had been some kind of rapport between them that was different from anything she'd ever known before. A handsome seducer with a sense of humour was a dangerous combination!

'I want to see the house.'

Dane's flat tones gave nothing away. She flicked a quick glance at his inscrutable face and heaved a resigned sigh. She might as well get used to the fact that she'd have to take people over the manor, much as she hated the idea.

'You'll keep your hands to yourself?'

'You bet I will,' he said sourly. 'Providing you don't come up with a pack of lies.'

'I don't need to lie about the house,' she said in a depressed tone, leading him past the little graveyard and Rose Cottage, where she lived. 'It's in a terrible state. You'll see for yourself.'

Even from the end of the drive, they could both see that she was right. The long grass on either side of the sentinel lime trees was scattered with poppies and blue scabious, creating a wild-looking foreground for the lovely lines of the Georgian manor house. But the paint was peeling and the portico collapsing. Broken window-sills and mouldings gave the house a sad, uncared-for air.

Dane extracted the details from his inside pocket and stood in the driveway, orientating himself.

'The fields to the left and right belong to Mrs Kendall, I see, and all the land down to the river.'

'That's right. The local farmer rents some.' Jade felt distinctly odd, pretending to be dispassionate.

'It says that some parts of the house are medieval. Which?'

A little taken aback by his businesslike snap, she bridled and then controlled herself, realising that he was probably already regretting the fact that he'd wasted his time coming down here. One look at the building had told him that it wasn't the wonderful 'snip' described in the brochure, after all. She needn't worry; he wouldn't like the house. He'd be looking for something smart to move into immediately, not a building which would need time, care and loving consideration for years to come.

'The cellars and the kitchen. And the dovecote.'

'Show me.'

Jade peered at the plan and stabbed her finger at the right place.

'That's been described as a studio, not the kitchens,' he puzzled.

'It's a big room, too big for a kitchen nowadays. You can see the conical roof from here,' she said, pointing. 'The smoke used to vent through the roof from a central cooking fire. It's been converted into a studio room. The new kitchens—well, Georgian ones—are on the other side of the dining-hall.'

He nodded and strode on, his black brows drawing closer and closer together as the extent of external disrepair became more evident.

'Who used the stuido?'

Jade started. 'Um . . . Mrs Kendall. Sketching, writing, that kind of thing.'

Thankfully he wasn't interested. Jade didn't want to launch into a discussion on the local history Mrs Kendall was writing! Dane King would probably sneer and think it would be an amateur attempt, and force her into defending the work, or even revealing who she was.

As they approached the front door, Jade felt increasingly nervous. He was the first person to be shown around, and she wasn't sure she could cope with the experience emotionally. For the past year she had avoided certain rooms, and only forced herself into the house when absolutely necessary. The big iron key grated in the lock and the door swung open to reveal a huge hall with its lovely oak floorboards and sweeping double staircase.

Dane took over. In fact, she didn't really know why she was there. He investigated everything thoroughly: testing for dry rot, jumping on floors, tapping plaster and shining his torch into dark corners. He would bring a torch! The lazy charmer was turning out to have another facet to his character: hard-headed businessman. He was quite a mixture, was Dane King!

As he poked and probed, muttered criticisms and frowned, Jade found the atmosphere of the house getting to her. Snatches of conversation, images, faces, lurked everywhere. A kind of sick misery dominated her mind as she relived incidents that she would have preferred to lie forgotten. And she grew more and more depressed, especially when he paused in front of the smashed shutters in the dining-room. But he made no comment. Jade remembered vividly when that had been done. But he spent some time frowning at the stains on the damask wallpaper. Her heart was in her mouth, waiting for his questions. He seemed about to speak and she steeled herself against the wash of shame that flooded her body, but he turned and walked into the hall and up the stairs, a thoughtful look on his face as he examined other evidence of careless damage.

Jade felt as though she had been reprieved. She stood outside the master bedroom, trying to control her emotions.

'Come on,' called Dane, examining the oak panelling. 'There's no charge to enter.'

Her eyes fell on the four-poster bed. Like most of the furniture and furnishings, it was being sold with the house. She wanted nothing to remind her of Sebastian. In her mind, she could visualise him, lying on the bed, waiting, his handsome face full of desire. Then the imagery was shattered as Dane sat on the mattress and read the particulars on the house carefully.

'For goodness' sake, come in,' he said, seeing her still shifting from one foot to the other. 'Tell me about this bed.'

'W-w-what?'

'How old it is.' His hands ran admiringly up the bulbous posts, tracing out the carvings.

'I believe it's 1680,' she replied distantly.

'Marvellous. To think of countless couples, drawing those curtains and making love . . .'

Pain lashed through Jade's body and she gave a small gasp, disguising it with a cough as Dane's eyes flicked in her direction.

'Lovely room.' He swung his legs up on to the bed and leaned back against the big headboard.

Jade was furious to see how relaxed and how *right* he looked there. He had no business to be so comfortable in her home, especially on that bed! Sebastian had bought it for her, to . . . Oh God! Would she never rid herself of this destructive memory? She whirled around and walked to the window, tense and emotionally distressed.

'I like the view,' he said softly.

Because of her tears, she was unable to answer, and it seemed he took her silence for encouragement.

'Why don't you come over here, Jade, and admire the room from where I am? I'm sure it's the best position from which to appreciate it.'

'Leave me alone!' she moaned, tipping her head back. 'You've had your fun. You've made a trip to the great outdoors, kissed a country girl and amused yourself criticising the run-down manor. That should be enough experiences to take back to provide entertainment for your chums in your club! Or at your next little drinkies party, or . . .'

She couldn't say any more, her throat was too constricted.

'Why don't you come clean?' he said quietly.

A brief fear flickered through her. He couldn't know! She started for the doorway with bowed head, letting her hair cover her distressed face.

'Stay where you are!' he rapped.

Jade nearly jumped out of her skin at the command. 'You . . . you bully!' she whispered. The lounging lizard had become a veritable tiger with bared teeth, and she was frightened.

'Well?' he asked menacingly.

'I don't know what you're talking about,' she began haughtily,.

'I've handled enough women in my time to know when they're upset or hiding something,' said Dane quietly.

She quivered with rage. Handled women, indeed! Male chauvinist. 'Yes, I'm hiding something! I'm trying to hide the fact that I don't like you,' she snapped.

'Maybe. But it's more than that. You don't want to sell the house, do you?'

'Of course I don't!' she cried. 'Would you? But I have to, I——' She stopped in mid-sentence. She'd fallen into his trap! Now he knew who she was! 'Oh, you swine,' she said bitterly. 'You tricked me!'

'It occurred to me that you might not willingly volunteer the information,' he said sardonically, rising and shutting the door firmly and standing in front of it.

'What . . . are . . . you doing?' she breathed, noting the grimness of his face and the determined ice of his blue eyes.

'Ensuring that you stop evading me,' he growled.

A shiver of sexual fear ran through her and he laughed mirthlessly. 'Don't tempt me,' he said huskily, his voice suddenly loaded with sensuality.

Jade recoiled at his arrogance. 'Tempt you? How dare you! Your conceit is beyond belief! Move away from that door!'

'Not until you tell me what you hoped to gain by

pretending to be the local school secretary, and getting everyone else in on the charade!'

'I *am* the secretary!' she said vehemently. 'I just didn't want anyone to know I . . .'

'You are Mrs Kendall?' he asked angrily.

'Yes.'

Regret tinged his face. 'You don't wear a ring,' he said tightly.

Jade bit her lip and slowly put the gold band back on her finger.

'You little fool!' he raged.

'I don't see why,' she lied, thinking however, how stupid she'd been.

'Don't you?' he muttered. 'If nothing else, didn't you realise that I would have been more considerate of your feelings while going round the house? It obviously upsets you to be here. I take it you are living in that cottage you mentioned: there are no personal things around.'

'Yes, I live in Rose Cottage next door,' she mumbled miserably.

'I suggest you get an agent to take over the house tours for you. Then you won't be plagued with painful memories of your late husband,' he said curtly.

'I——' Jade rocked on her feet.

'God!' He moved forwards to her, then stopped, regarding her helplessly. She struggled for composure and then turned and threw herself on the bed, sobbing uncontrollably.

'Mrs Kendall, Jade . . .'

'Go away!' she yelled through her tears, petrified that he'd try to comfort her. She was so muddled and confused that she couldn't stand sympathy right now. She was too vulnerable, and might tell this total stranger everything about herself. In despair she buried her face in the pillow, and to her utter relief he obeyed her. She heard the door shut and then a silence.

The tears fell unchecked as if they'd been stored up behind a dam. Jade hadn't cried for years, not even after her parents had died when she was twenty-three. They'd been enjoying one of their frequent holidays when an overloaded ferry sank in a Chinese harbour, killing everyone on board—her parents included. Numb with shock, and unable to deal with the muddled finances, Jade had turned to her current boyfriend, Sebastian. He'd handled everything. Still numb, she found herself married to him.

'Oh, Sebastian!' she moaned aloud.

She wept even more copiously, full of self-pity that she was having to sell Saxonbury and was forced to show devious men like Dane King around it. By the time she had cried herself out and rolled over on to her back, it was almost dusk.

The bed suddenly depressed and she screamed with fright, wrenching her neck around to see that it was Dane.

'What are you doing here? When did you come back?' she asked belligerently, sitting up and trying to conceal the effects of her crying bout.

'I didn't leave. I was in the house all the time.'

She looked at him in horror. 'All the time?'

'Yes. I thought you oughtn't to be left alone,' he said quietly. 'I felt you needed someone. I explored the rest of the house and came back. You were crying so much you didn't even hear. Poor Jade. All this is hitting you very badly, isn't it?'

His hand stretched out and pushed her heavy, damp hair away from her face, then he reached to the side-table and she saw to her astonishment that he had found a bowl and filled it with ice-cold water. He dipped his pale gold handkerchief into this and gently bathed her face.

Jade relaxed, welcoming the cool relief. An occasional sob broke from her trembling lips, and Dane gripped her hand in sympathy.

'Better?' he asked in concern.

She nodded, feeling limp.

'You must have loved your husband very much,' he murmured. 'I envy you. It's something to cherish. You're lucky to have had such a relationship.'

Jade couldn't speak. Her big melting eyes focused on Dane's broad shoulder, and suddenly she flung her arms around his neck and held on tightly.

'It's OK,' he soothed, his hand stroking her back. 'I understand now. You've been upset because I ignorantly waded into a situation that I misread, and I apologise. But you did set it up, you know. You're as much to blame, and you must be straight with people in future or you'll be hurt again.'

'I know,' she muttered, wishing she didn't find him so damnably attractive. She must be in a highly emotional state! Her mouth longed to move forwards one little inch and taste his smooth golden neck. She discovered that her hands were playing with his hair and willed them to be still.

Then he was lifting her away and she was saved from making any foolish moves.

'I'll walk you home and we'll talk there,' he said briskly.

'Talk?'

'About my offer.'

'But . . .'

'Let's get you home, shall we?' he suggested. 'This bedroom is no place to stay, for either of us.'

With a shock, Jade realised from the desire in his eyes

and the curve of his mouth that he still wanted to kiss her, despite the matter-of-fact tone. Stunned, her eyes searched his and after a moment he averted his gaze and strode quickly to the door, holding it open.

Jade slowly got up and stumbled. In a flash, his arm was around her waist and he was helping her to walk along the landing and down the stairs, his face very grim.

She was grateful for his support and totally unnerved by her uncharacteristic fragility. His hip was warm against hers and she had to steel herself not to push into him. What on earth was the matter with her? How had this skilful, experienced Don Juan managed to wheedle his way under her defences? Her mind seemed to be the consistency of treacle; nothing made sense any more. She oughtn't to be clutching this man and wishing he was kissing her instead. She should have told him, sharply that she wouldn't sell Saxonbury to him, and sent him packing.

Yet he had taken command of the situation and, although he didn't know it, had temporarily taken command of her senses. She groaned inwardly. It must be something to do with delayed shock. She needed a man to lean on and he was available. Jade despised herself for being so feeble. All her life she'd been fiercely independent, apart from that very understandable helplessness when her parents had died. Now history was repeating itself, but this time the man wasn't single and she hadn't know him for six months as she had known Sebastian.

'Which way?'

'Left.' They had reached the end of the drive and turned towards her cottage. 'I can manage now,' she muttered.

'Nonsense. I'll make you a cup of tea and then we'll sort things out. You really are in quite a state inside, Jade.'

'I was all right till you kissed me,' she said waspishly.

He frowned. 'Yes. I can't tell you how sorry I am about that. I'd give anything not to have touched you,' he said in a low-pitched voice.

'You do have a conscience, then,' she muttered.

'You're at a dangerous stage,' he growled.

She was, she thought wistfully. Her year of marriage with Sebastian had made her terribly susceptible to men like Dane King. She took in a deep, controlling breath and walked on.

It was a balmy spring evening. Flocks of starlings swept the darkening sky as they returned to roost in the lime trees. Jade's prize cockerel crowed in the still air and was answered by the thin scream of a vixen, somewhere in the woods. The scent of lilac and May blossom was overpoweringly sweet, and Jade knew she could never leave Saxonbury village. She would come to terms with her new life in the little cottage and bury herself in her work. This would be the year that she finished her most challenging book yet.

In the fading light, Jade noticed that one of the red roses clambering up her cottage wall had opened that afternoon; soon the rest would follow and the flinty stone would be bright with scarlet splashes.

'Aptly named cottage,' remarked Dane, following her eyes. 'Are you going to let me come in and make sure you're settled?'

'You sound like a bossy nurse,' sighed Jade, motioning him inside nevertheless.

'I'm making tea, not tucking you into bed,' he said, then his brows drew together in an angry line and he made much of taking off his jacket and draping it over the back of her favourite armchair. 'Kitchen?'

She showed him into the big, airy room with its bleached

wood table and chairs and old oak dresser sporting what remained of the family china.

'You go and sit down,' he said. 'You'll be under my feet.'

'I have to feed my dog, Polly,' she said, wondering why her retriever hadn't barked as she usually did. Jade prepared the dog food and then stood in the back doorway, calling, growing more and more worried that Polly didn't come.

'Trouble?' Dane looked down at her anxious face.

'Maybe. Sometimes she leaves the garden and wanders the manor land, but never goes anywhere else.'

'I'll go and look.'

'It's almost dark—you'll fall over things . . .'

'Then I'll have to get up, won't I?'

She frowned. 'Why are you being so nice?'

'It's my role in life to help females in trouble.'

'How gallant,' she said drily.

'Don't knock it,' he snapped. 'You need me at this moment.'

'Like hell I do!' she cried, unwilling to accept the truth of what he said. Having him take over was lovely. She'd been fighting on her own for so long now and was tired, physically and emotionally.

'Then go find your own damn dog!' he snarled, losing patience and turning on his heel.

Resignedly, Jade did just that, the sound of a kettle and crockery being clattered about receding as she made her way down the dark garden. She looked back and saw him silhouetted in the golden glow from the kitchen window; apparently watching her.

Jade plunged on, disconcerted by the secure feeling he gave her by being there, in her cottage. Then her distracted mind was alerted to the sound of whimpering. Her pulses

racing, she clambered over the low wall at the back and into
the manor field which ran down to the river, scattering
browsing rabbits as she ran. What she saw, when she
reached the bank, made her heart turn over. Polly had just
succeeded in drawing her leg from a poacher's trap.

'Polly! Oh, you poor thing!' cried Jade, as the dog tried to
limp towards her on three legs. She prevented Polly from
moving any more, holding her tightly and stroking her. The
leg looked dreadfully torn, and Jade averted her eyes from
the sight, feeling a mixture of sickness and fury. She had to
get a grip on herself and carry Polly back somehow.

Helplessly she assessed the dog's weight: too much for
her, but she'd have to manage.

'Jade? Where are you?'

Dane—he was strong enough! 'Over here! Hurry! Please
hurry! Polly's hurt!'

She heard him running and then saw him with an
incredible sense of relief, his eyes blazing with anger when
he saw the retriever's plight.

Cursing softly, he placed a reassuring hand on Jade's
shoulder and knelt to examine the bleeding leg. His mouth
in a hard, tight line, he rose, uprooted the spring trap and
flung it furiously into the deep waters of the river, where it
slowly sank without trace into the deep mud at the bottom.

'It probably looks worse than it is,' he said. 'But she may
have damaged her tendons as well as the muscle. I'll carry
her to my car. Is there a vet nearby?'

'Lewes. I'll have to ring,' she said, bobbing along
anxiously beside him and intermittently soothing Polly.

'Do you often let her roam free?' he asked tightly.

'No! That is—she's always had the freedom of Saxonbury
Manor land.'

'If children play there, you'd better get the police to

find the poacher. There could be a nasty accident.'

'Will she be all right?' she asked, upset.

'She'll get over it, don't worry. In a couple of weeks you'll never know she hurt herself at all. Dogs are more resilient than people,' he added, half to himself.

What an odd thing to say, thought Jade, acknowledging that he was probably right. Perhaps he was alluding to the fact that he thought she was still mourning the loss of her husband.

Dane had to drive to the town. Jade held Polly all the way as he raced at speed along the narrow country lane, controlling the car with expert hands. The vet confirmed Dane's opinion that the injury looked worse than it was.

'What will you do to her?' she asked, trembling and white, Dane's supportive arm around her shoulders.

'We'll give her an anaesthetic and antibiotics, and repair the damaged muscles,' said the vet. 'As far as I can see, no major muscle is affected and the tendons are fine, though we'll have a proper look tomorrow under the anaesthetic.'

'When do we collect her?' asked Dane.

Jade felt oddly at home in the shelter of his friendly arm, and comforted in the way he had said 'we'. She was feeling so shaky that she needed his strength.

'I'll ring you. She'll be almost normal in ten days or so, depending on what we find, of course,' said the vet reassuringly. 'Leave her with me and don't worry.'

'Thank you,' said Jade, and stroked Polly's head for a moment.

'I think you ought to get home,' said Dane. 'You look drained.'

With a final gentle hug for Polly and a grateful handclasp for the vet, Jade allowed Dane to escort her to his car and settle her in the passenger seat. All the way home he kept up an inconsequential—and rather one-sided—conversation about driving in the country or on motorways, and she was glad that her mind was occupied.

But when they arrived, and it was time for her to thank him and say goodbye, she felt a sudden panic at the idea of never seeing him again. Oh, Jade, you fool! she moaned to herself. Don't get tangled up with him!

He sat in the car, not moving, looking out at her cottage. 'This must be very different to your house,' she blurted out, curious to know something of his life-style.

'Very,' he smiled. 'I have a penthouse suite in the City.'

Her heart sank, He *was* a City slicker, then. 'Still, ideal for entertaining, parties and so on,' she probed.

'Ideal.' His tone gave nothing away, but, as Jade looked at his perfect profile, she saw how hard his expression was and knew from the set of his jaw that he would be as ruthless in love as he was in business. Then he swept her with lazy eyes, an invitation in his glance, and she stiffened.

'Aren't you going to ask me in?' he murmured.

'Certainly not!' she flushed.

'I could do with a coffee before I go.'

She'd heard that excuse rather too often for it to sway her. Then she felt churlish. After all, he had put himself out for Polly—though he was probably like all Englishmen, and had a soft spot for dogs.

'A quick coffee, then. I'm awfully tired.'

He lowered his eyes and slid out of his seat, coming around to open the door for her. Emotionally exhausted, she was hardly able to raise the energy to get out of the car.

'When did you last eat anything?' asked Dane shrewdly, as she listlessly opened her front door.

'Um . . . I think it must have been breakfast. You took over my lunch hour,' she complained.

'Sit down,' he said gently, thrusting her into an armchair. 'Everything's happened today, hasn't it?' he said softly, crouching down and taking her hand.

'Stop being so *nice!*' she moaned, longing to lose herself against his friendly-looking chest.

He smiled. 'Shall I yell at you?'

'Yes,' she said sulkily. That way, she could hate him, although then she would have to feel ashamed of the way her body responded when he looked at her with his sultry eyes.

'I'll make us some supper instead,' he said drily.

Her nerves jangled every time he made a noise in the kitchen. She had to get a grip on herself! She didn't need anyone. She could cope. Once she'd eaten something she'd feel fine. But she didn't. He brought in scrambled eggs on toast and a dish of strawberries. Famished, she tucked into the meal with a quick expression of thanks, and didn't speak until she'd swallowed the last delicious strawberry.

'I don't want to push you,' he said tentatively, 'but I ought to be going, and . . .'

'Oh, yes. I've kept you. Do you want to ring home?' Her voice was suddenly hard as she remembered his situation. He'd shown a remarkable lack of consideration for his wife, who was probably patiently waiting with a dinner burning in the oven.

'No. Jade, let me make things easy for you. I want to buy Saxonbury and can come to some agreement with you now and finalise the arrangement tomorrow. That would save you any more distress in showing people the house, and you wouldn't have to go through the strain of the auction. How about it?'

She bit her lip and imagined what it would be like to having him living next door, bumping into her in the street, chairing the parish council, running the Garland Day Show

with her. And his wife. She knew enough about her
rocketing emotions and his evident interest in her to know
that his presence would bring trouble. He was a charming
lecher, ready to flirt and seduce any likely female who came
his way—he'd proved that today. She seemed to be so
starved of affection and the pleasure of being touched that
she couldn't answer for her behaviour any more. No way
would she come between a man and his wife, even if the
wife was already being betrayed.

'I will not sell to you,' she said huskily, denying herself
what she wanted more than anything at the moment.

'Jade.' He sat on the arm of her chair and placed his
hands on either side of her. 'I realise you're shaken by the
things that happened this afternoon. The way I walked
around your ex-home, Polly, my attitude towards you
personally. But you must think. I'm making a good offer.'

'No.' She wouldn't meet his gaze. He was being too
gentle, too careful of her feelings. She wanted him to be
unpleasant.

'Why are you so against me?' he asked. 'I acted badly, I
know, but you are rather irresistible, and I am keeping my
hands off you now,' he said with an engaging grin. 'Since
then I've been rather well behaved and helpful, haven't I?'

'Dane, this is a quiet backwater. You'd stick out like a
sore thumb in your knife-edge trousers and carefully
moulded jacket. This isn't a suitable place to amuse
yourself on weekends with Yuppies and Sloanes or whizz-
kid stockbrokers. I have no wish to live next door to
someone who holds wild orgies, or to see nude bathing in
the river, or to be woken in the early hours by cavalcades of
sports cars roaring in the drive, or . . .'

'Nor do I,' he said, amused. 'What references can *you*
give?'

'Me? Why, you——'

'Outrageous, isn't it? Yet you blindly accuse me of the most extraordinary behaviour without any grounds at all.'

'I know your sort . . .' she began.

'No, you don't!' he said, exasperated. 'Don't pre-judge people. I'm surprised at you. I took you for a woman who has an open mind and is free of prejudice. It seems I was wrong.'

He kept boxing her into corners, making her say things she didn't really mean, making her sound narrow. Jade didn't like that. But she was really scared that he'd bring his sophisticated morality to the house next door. That would drive her out. One year of flagrant immoral behaviour was enough, without having it repeated. She was furious with Dane for bringing it all back in her mind. But for him, that time would be almost forgotten.

'Thank you for everything you've done for me,' she whispered. 'I'm very tired and I have to be up early in the morning. Will you go now?'

'If you think you'll be all right, yes. Let me have your number and I'll ring you tomorrow when you're feeling more like talking business.'

Jade was relieved that he had risen and was intending to go at last. She wouldn't lose her self-respect by having her body thrown into turmoil by his extraordinary sensuality any longer. He reached for his jacket and slipped it on, looking tense, and Jade's heart lurched foolishly. She'd have to put him off for good.

'You're not very good at taking hints, are you?' she said coldly. 'Get it into your thick skull, Mr King: I have a particular kind of buyer in mind for Saxonbury. A family, with loads of children. I imagine you don't have any children?'

'Not that I know of,' he bit out.

'Oh, I'm sure there are a few scattered around, growing up to charm women just like their father,' she said scathingly. 'Forget all ideas of moving here. I'll withdraw the house if it looks as if you'd be its owner. I'd rather see the place rot then let you take possession!'

'Rot?' he growled. 'Not if I can help it. Start getting used to the idea of me in that bed of yours.' His eyes blazed with an odd light and Jade felt a tingle spreading down her spine. 'I'll take possession. You can count on that!'

CHAPTER THREE

'YOU ready, Jade?'

I'm ready, she thought. I've been ready for hours. 'Yes, Charlie, just coming!' she called out of her bedroom window, smiling down on the big blacksmith. Charlie was one big hunk of a man and had sent the village girls into raptures ever since he'd donned long trousers. He was thirty now, about Dane King's age, she mused, then her eyes darkened. Charlie was different. He wasn't married and he was honest.

She paused in front of her mirror. The bright orange shirt and long, flowing skirt were her fourth change of clothes. She looked a bit like a lollipop! Her face was better for the grin, and she decided to enjoy the day and think of the money that would come at the end of it.

Grabbing a brown suede shoulder-bag, tying a citrus-yellow ribbon on top of her head and teasing her hair into casual disarray around it, she rushed down to Charlie.

'You're a knockout,' he said admiringly, as she flung the door open.

Jade beamed and caught hold of his hesitantly offered hand. 'And you are doing wonders to my self-confidence,' she said gratefully.

'You don't need that,' he said in his slow, lovely brogue. 'You know you're the most beautiful woman in Sussex.'

'Charlie!' she laughed, flushing at the compliment. 'You're an angel. I feel a million dollars. I'm so glad you're going to keep an eye on me today. You will stop me if

I start to cry, or get indignant, or . . .'

'I'll stop you, Jade,' he grinned. 'Though I'm not telling you as how I'll do it.'

Oh dear, she thought sadly. He was getting the wrong idea. Though, if Dane King did decide to turn up, Charlie would be about the most intimidating defence she could muster. Her eyes slanted at the enormous biceps straining the too-tight T-shirt and lifted to Charlie's massive, solid jaw. He'd look after her, and she'd make sure she gently let him know that she wasn't in the market for any kind of boyfriend.

Dane had rung the next day, but only to ask about Polly, who was doing fine and would be allowed to leave the following afternoon. He was very polite and cool and never mentioned the house at all, so Jade was able to relax, knowing he'd either discussed it with his wife and she'd vetoed the idea, or he'd thought better of it.

Many people had visited the house prior to the auction, though she'd taken Dane's advice and asked the estate agent to handle all that. Jade was determined not to get involved, and her only contribution had been to direct two very nice-looking couples to Saxonbury. Her mornings were taken up with the school, her afternoons with looking after the fantails at the manor, her own livestock and garden. Most evenings she managed to settle down to working on her book, and was pleased with the research she had done so far, using many of the old volumes kept in the manor library which had been handed down by successive owners.

There would be another owner by the end of the afternoon. Her small hand, dwarfed by Charlie's large paw, grew limp at the thought, and he gave it a reassuring squeeze when they saw the cars lining the driveway. Then, as they made their way up the stone steps to the dilapidated

door, she heard a sound that she recognised: Dane's car.
Charlie corrected her slight stumble by placing his arm
around her small waist. As they entered, she half turned,
unable to prevent herself looking to see whether Dane had
noticed the gesture.

It seemed he had. He was standing by the car, glaring.
Jade felt triumphant that she had shown him she was now
strong and carefree, and couldn't be manipulated by him as
on that fateful day when they met. But inside, she knew that
the sudden flip of her stomach and the warm glow that
followed had nothing to do with the way Charlie looked at
her, nor was her body responding to his gently stroking
fingers. If Dane had been touching her like that, her nerves
would be singing. Even the thought was making her tingle.
Jade's eyes blazed with anger at herself. Dane King was a
no-good, worthless seducer, far too accomplished in the arts
of lovemaking to be satisfied with her for long. She wasn't
in the market for that kind of man.

'Are you all right, Jade?' asked Charlie anxiously,
bending a tender head towards her.

Grimly she pulled herself together. 'It's a bit odd, coming
to watch people bid for your home. I feel rather light-
headed.'

'Wish I had the money to buy it,' he said wistfully. 'I'd
give it to you like a shot.'

'You are a darling,' she said warmly. For a moment she
thought she heard a low murmur behind her, but her
attention was diverted by the auctioneer.

'Good turnout, Mrs Kendall,' he said, his gleaming eyes
assessing the crowd. 'We should making a killing today.'

She bit back her dislike of the man. After all, she needed
to make money as much as he needed his commission: it
was no good getting on her high horse and scorning his

attitude. Somehow she had to pay her mounting debts.

'I hope you'll get the best price you can,' she said, managing a smile.

'For you,' said the man admiringly, 'I'll pull out all the stops.'

Jade was suddenly pulled tightly against Charlie's brawny chest. She looked up to see that he was glaring at the auctioneer, and suppressed a rueful smile.

'Perhaps we'd better make our way down to the front,' she suggested hastily. 'You won't forget to check with me before you take the final bid, will you?'

'No, I won't,' assured the man, ostentatiously clearing a path through the throng for her.

The auction was being held in the spacious drawing-room, but even that hadn't proved large enough for the crowd which had gathered. The doors at the far end had been opened right back so that the temporary benches could be arranged right down the long gallery. A massive, battered table provided a stage for the auctioneer, who now clambered up to a desk, perched on top, and for a few moments surveyed the room with a critical, practised eye, searching out likely buyers and separating them from the mere onlookers.

Most of the villagers were there, determined not to miss the entertainment, but they were genuinely sympathetic towards Jade and she felt she was among friends. It was a bit like a royal progress, she thought, making her way towards the front, where a seat had been reserved for her. Charlie made the most of the crush, by holding her in a protective way; he was taking his duties seriously!

The back of her neck was prickling, her imagination seeing Dane watching her like a hawk. She became very nervous, wondering if she'd have the nerve to stop the auction if he made the last bid. It would cause such a commotion! Then she smiled to herself. With Charlie beside her, no one would question her decision! And that would be one big surprise for the confident Mr King.

As usual with any meeting, there were few people on the front bench, and her 'reserved' sticker had been unnecessary. She allowed Charlie to keep his arm around her, but shot him a gently disapproving glance when his hand began to wander over her hip.

'Not the time or the place,' she smiled, not wanting to hurt him.

'Later?' he queried, his big face serious.

Still looking up at Charlie, she was aware that someone had come to sit next to her, and she automatically moved closer to Charlie to make room because the bench was filling up. She gazed into his hopeful eyes and smiled, thinking how open and straightforward he was. This was a man you could be sure of, one who was already half-way to adoring her. Starved of love and genuine affection—not the Dane King sort, she thought with asperity—she liked the calm feeling of stolid reliability about Charlie. Her smile broadened into an encouraging invitation, wishing he could stir her senses.

'Well, I'm celebrating in the pub tonight, if you want to be there,' she said.

His eyes lit up. 'Fantastic. It's a date.'

'Hello, Jade. How's Polly?' drawled a honeyed voice beside her.

Jade stiffened and immediately felt the acceleration in her pulse-rate. How on earth did he do it to her? she thought resentfully, edging even closer to Charlie.

'Fine, thank you,' she said with a cold politeness.

'Good. And . . . you?'

How could someone imbue ordinary words with so much

meaningful sensuality? Jade's nervousness increased. Sensing the way she trembled, Charlie's hand moved to grip her bare arm and he hugged her.

'Can I get you a glass of water, or something?' he asked in a worried voice.

To her annoyance, Dane had already sized up the situation and walked forwards to the auctioneer's table, commandeering one of the glasses on it. He handed it to her without a word, his face inscrutable.

For a moment she stared at the water, not wanting to take it for one stupid, irrational moment, and then gratefully gulped it down before handing it back with a brief and rather ungracious thanks.

'My pleasure,' said Dane mockingly, returning the glass.

Before he had resumed to his seat, there was a stir at the rear of the hall, and while Jade stared fixedly ahead Charlie turned and gave a low whistle.

'High society's just arrived,' he whispered loudly in Jade's ear.

As her head lifted to look, she caught sight of Dane, who seemed to recognise whoever was making everyone chatter excitedly, and with a terrible pang she knew that it must be his wife. Her teeth clenched together in a resolve to get her wayward emotions under control.

He looked delighted. There was love in his eyes. Tenderness. Jade shut out his expression, diverted by the need to cope with the fierce, searing stabs of jealousy that tore through her body. The intensity of her reaction terrified her: she'd built up Dane's effect on her out of all proportion; she'd dwelt on him too much; she was vulnerable at the moment and he'd taken her by storm with his suave, incomparably smooth approach. She had no right to feel jealous. Nothing had happened between them—only a paltry kiss.

And yet . . . she'd been drawn to him inexorably, as if they had been magnetised. If Dane had only been a surface charmer, she would have been able to reject him as a shallow flirt. Unfortunately for her, he'd shown other, more attractive sides to his character, and she had to admit that even now, with his wife approaching closer and closer every second, she wanted to know more about him, talk to him, enjoy his company. She was insane. For too long emotions had ruled her life. Half-Italian she might be, but she was also half-British, and that was what she ought to be cultivating at this moment. She had to be sensible and realise that a girl like her ought to seek a steady man like Charlie.

'Darling!'

Husky tones, warm and loving, and sincere, were being spoken by a woman bearing down on Dane. Jade was dimly aware of a pale gold silk skirt brushing past her, and then her eyes flickered up. Dane was fondly embracing a gorgeous redhead, whose hair had been knotted under a tiny tip-tilted hat which matched her silk suit. She had a stunning figure—all curves—and she used it to great effect. The people all around were riveted.

'How was the flight?' he asked his wife.

'I've no idea,' she purred. 'I was drinking champagne all the way.'

Dean looked elated. 'Does that mean you've got Dorothy for me?'

'On a plate, darling. She's breathless with eager anticipation for your magic touch.'

Jade's mouth fell open. Surely she couldn't have heard that properly! Some of Sebastian's friends had been unbelievably casual in their morals, but this . . . She'd

thought Dane was a practised deceiver, but his whole life-
style sounded more decadent than she dreamt of!

'I'll do the same for you one day,' he murmured, sitting
next to Jade and drawing his wife to the seat beside him.
The episode had firmed Jade's mind, both in connection
with denying him the manor, and denying him any physical
access to herself. She felt the same disgust that had
permeated her life during her brief marriage. That settled
it: Dane King would not own Saxonbury; she would not see
a potentially lovely house used as an entertainment centre
for sexually jaded jet-setters.

Seeing his wife was actually quite a relief. Now there
would be no more twinges of desire for him. Even if she'd
wanted to, she couldn't hold a candle to such a beauty. It
was clear that Dane adored his wife and found her totally
irresistible, from the way his eyes had admired the way she
looked, and Jade could only surmise that he was highly
sexed and used other women to sate his lust during Mrs
King's absences, or to revive a tired palate. She'd known of
people like that herself, after all.

Holding fiercely on to her pride, she ostentatiously patted
Charlie's knee, wanting Dane to know that it meant nothing
to her to see him with his wife. Charlie closed his hand over
hers and nodded towards the auctioneer. He was ready to
begin.

Using a map to remind the potential buyers of the extent
of the estate, and eulogising over the surrounding
countryside, he launched into a brief résumé of the house
and it's contents, then listed the barons of Saxonbury from
the Norman Conquest in 1066. Jade felt the sensation of
pride quiver in her as it had when she had first learnt of the
house's history, and remembered how bitterly she had
resented its defilement.

Bidding began slowly, no one apparently wishing to make the early play. Jade was on the edge of her seat, petrified that the reserve price wouldn't be reached—she couldn't go through this day again. What on earth would she do?

'Two hundred thousand . . .'

Jade saw the auctioneer's glance had picked up a bid from Dane and she froze.

'I've come to buy. You didn't think I was here just to see you, did you?' murmured Dane's amused voice in her ear.

As she glared at him, he nodded at the auctioneer and the price went up again.

'Stop bidding!' she seethed. 'There's no point. I won't let you have Saxonbury. I won't have you living in this village.'

'You will have me, Jade. Wait and see,' he said out of the corner of his mouth.

She flashed him a look of blazing hatred and set her mouth, worried that only a few were countering his bids. She held Charlie's hand very tightly, aware that Dane was eyeing her whitened knuckles.

Slowly the price rose. Others came into the bidding. Every time the auctioneer looked at Dane, Jade's stomach turned over. Gradually, the atmosphere grew tense. Five interested parties were battling it out. Despite being in a state of disrepair, the house hadn't reached the state of no return—it had only been neglected for about eighteen months, after all—and the estate with its woods, meadows and river frontage was highly desirable.

Then Jade realised that it was a long time since Dane had made a bid. She risked looking in his direction; he met her eyes and gave a regretful shrug. Her sense of overpowering relief was replaced by triumph, and her face filled with joy. He couldn't afford her house! He would slide out of her

life and go back to corrupting City girls! Jade flashed him a
grin of pure delight and settled down to enjoy herself, all
her worries evaporating.

The price had risen above the reserve, and Jade caught
auction fever, sharing with Charlie the elation she felt.
She'd be solvent at last, the debts paid, and would have
enough money to live comfortably. What a relief!

Beside her, Dane was relaxing in evident defeat. Few
were bidding now, and then the auctioneer's eagle eye was
darting between the only two people left in the running.

To Jade's left was a genial-faced elderly man in brown
cords and a well-worn jumper. He appeared to have a
number of relatives with him: an extended family by the
looks of it. He was bidding against a rosy-cheeked woman
joggling a little boy on her knee.

'OK?' asked Charlie, seeing Jade's brilliant eyes.

'Yes,' she whispered. 'I like either of those two, don't
you?'

'I'm so glad you're happy, Jade.'

He leant his head affectionately against hers. Dane's legs
stretched out languidly in their beige linen and were noisily
crossed. Jade tried not to giggle at the childish gesture as he
drew attention to himself. He just didn't like any woman
being uninterested in him! And under that laconic exterior
he must be seething mad not to be in a position to crow over
her in victory!

The auctioneer was whipping up interest by his quickfire
delivery. The whole of Jade's body was strung taut with
electrified vitality, her face alive with fierce anticipation.
Someone caring would take Saxonbury and that was all she
wanted—apart from enough money to live on!

Tension mounted as the auctioneer took advantage of a
pause to hype the house and encourage further bidders.

Jade wished he wouldn't. Dane might be swayed by the rhetoric. But he remained nonchalant, almost indifferent.

'. . . incomparable setting in the Ouse valley, set in magnificent grounds besides a church nearly a thousand years old and in one of the most picturesque . . .'

Jade felt on top of the world. It *was* a heavenly place to live, and she'd still be there, in the valley, even if she didn't have the space she once enjoyed. In a way it was just as well that she couldn't afford to live in Saxonbury. At least she wouldn't be haunted by its memories.

'. . . the bid is with the lady in the front row. Going once . . .' The auctioneer glanced at the elderly man, who shook his head ruefully. 'Going twice . . .' He stared directly at Jade, as he had been instructed, in case she objected. She beamed happily, unable to contain her delight. A woman with a family. The gavel banged down. 'Sold to the lady in the front row. Your name, please, madam?'

The woman stood, placing the toddler on his feet. At the same time, Dane King rose.

'She is acting for me,' he said smoothly. 'Dane King.'

'Would you give me details of yourself, Mr King?'

Jade was momentarily paralysed with shock. She couldn't believe her ears. *Dane?* The owner? He'd dropped out of the bidding, he'd . . . Oh, God! Her horrified gasp was heard by everyone in the room. In hushed interest, Dane strode to the table, already writing out the cheque for the ten per cent deposit as he went, while Jade watched, quite numb. He'd tricked her—again! Of all the slimy, devious . . .

'Jade, what's . . .'

She wrenched herself free from Charlie's restricting grip and marched grimly up to Dane, conscious that the whole of the village, and perfect strangers, were watching avidly.

'Cancel the sale,' she hissed to the auctioneer. 'I will not sell my home to this man!'

'Jade . . .'

'Leave me alone, Charlie!' she muttered.

'You said I had to stop you if . . .'

Jade stiffened at Dane's amused chuckle. He scrawled his signature on the contract held out by her solicitor, but she hardly noticed what he was doing in her anger. How dared he make fun of her!

'Don't push me, Mr King, or I'll set him on you. He's the local blacksmith, you know.'

'I'm afraid muscles don't cut much ice in law,' he said urbanely.

'What law?' she snapped.

'The law that says the auction is legally binding once contracts have been exchanged. This is yours, I think. You shouldn't have pre-signed it; that was very foolish. I'm sure your solicitor advised against it.'

He had. Jade groaned inwardly, realising that her attempt to minimise her involvement on the day of the auction had backfired on her. In twenty-eight days, Dane would be in the manor.

The solicitor nodded. 'You've sold to Mr King,' he said, rubbing salt into Jade's wounds. 'He can take possession any time he wants when the month is up.'

'Possession. The idea is exciting,' murmured Dane huskily, his mouth wickedly sensual. 'I shall enjoy that enormously.'

She flung him a withering look. 'There's nothing I can do?' she asked the auctioneer bitterly.

'Well, no, but you wouldn't want to, surely? It's a very good price. Excuse me, I have to attend the Fat Stock show. I'll be in touch. Goodbye,' he said, shaking everyone's hand.

'Cheer up,' said Charlie, putting his hand on her shoulder. 'What does it matter who lives there? Your cottage is smashing. Why don't you let me make a fence for you to stop Polly wandering? I'd do it free of charge.'

She was defeated. Jade saw Dane's mocking look as he waited for her reply, and a devil within her made her lips curve invitingly at Charlie.

'That's a wonderful idea! Come back and measure up now, would you?' she said warmly. 'Then I can get us a snack and we can celebrate however we like. Any ideas?' Her brows arched saucily, though her heart felt like lead.

'Plenty,' said Charlie enthusiastically, hardly able to believe his luck.

'Goodbye, Mr King,' she said coolly. 'I do hope you don't invite me to any of your parties. I have to say that I am now one of yours most ardent enemies.'

With a careless smile in his direction, and totally ignoring the gorgeous redhead, who was chatting animatedly to the woman who had bid for the Kings, Jade slid her arm around Charlie and walked out with him, her legs shaking uncontrollably. Luckily no one could see how unsteady she was; her long skirts hid the evidence.

She'd never felt less like celebrating in her life, but she did, passing a tolerably pleasant afternoon, forcing herself to face up to facts and plan a life for herself that didn't include any wistful longing for the excitement that Dane King had to offer. But, although she tried hard to be fair on Charlie and give him a chance, she did find his lack of sparkle unappealing. He was a wonderful man, she thought, as he kissed her goodnight at her front door, after an evening in the Vine, but not for her. Alas, she'd been reared on a much more exotic diet. Her life with her parents had spoiled her for stolid, ordinary men. That was the trouble: the most interesting men were always the most wicked. And, she sighed, often married!

Jade couldn't understand why her mind persisted in drifting off and flashing images of Dane and his sultry mouth at her. Despite her mother's frantic and Bohemian life, it had also been a very moral one and typical of a woman from a strongly bonded Naples family. Jade had learnt to respect family ties and was naturally loyal. As she grew up into a young woman, she unquestioningly accepted the idea that marriage was for ever, and faithfulness went with that. Of course you were faithful to your husband and he to you. Any man or woman who sought to break up a marriage, or to have an affair, was beneath contempt.

So how could she even remember with enjoyment the way Dane had kissed her? And, worse still, why did she forget so readily that she was just another in a long line of eager women? How was it that all her efforts to shut him out of her mind were proving to be fruitless?

She was disappointed in herself. Obviously her latent sensuality was wayward and needed a stern talking-to. Then she brightened up. Perhaps everyone had temptations. It was all a question of determination and time. Once she was involved in demanding work and had a steady relationship, then she'd look back on this ridiculous infatuation and laugh.

It seemed only a short while before the village street was busy with contractor's lorries, delivery vans and smart coupés driven by businesslike women whom Jade took to be interior decorators. Mrs Love had discovered that the new owner was Dane King of the King Literary Agency, a huge international organisation which represented some of the most famous and lucrative authors in the world.

The villagers were pleased, hoping it would bring publicity and boost attendance at Barlock Weir's house.

It was in a bad state of repair and, although the parish council owned it, they might have to sell it to the National Trust. This summer, all the proceeds of the Garland Day fête would go towards the fund for the house.

Occasionally Dane turned up in his sleek black car, looking sleek and black himself in his dark business suits, investigating the work being done at the manor. Jade avoided him assiduously.

Knowing that he'd visited Saxonbury the day before, she felt safe in taking one of her favourite short walks along the riverbank one afternoon. She left Polly behind, since the swans were nesting as usual in the brook running to the Ouse.

Rooks spiralled above the elm trees, hopefully eyeing the newly shorn sheep and their lambs in the pastures below. Thick, puffy clouds hung over Firle Beacon, a dark green, wedge-shaped hill on the horizon. Contentedly she sniffed the air. Old flint barns belonging to the manor, their roofs open to the sky, had become overgrown with wild Russian vine, the huge white swathes of blossom drifting daintily in the gentle breeze. Jade stopped to watch the majestic swans gliding through the silvered river, and crossed the little bridge.

Ahead, beyond the field of young green barley, stood the great stand of horse-chestnut trees, holding their flowers aloft like white candles. But in them something was rustling. Jade frowned, wondering if it was a poacher.

'Miss!'

It was Billy! Like most small boys, he ignored marital status and always called her 'miss'. Jade grinned. He must be stuck. Then she was proved wrong, as he thudded to the ground and ran up to her.

'It's my kitten, miss. She's up the tree and won't come

down,' he explained, his cheery face grubby with tears.

She walked to the tree and cast an expert eye over it, searching for the best way up.

'Will you stand here, miss, while I run and get help?'

'What's wrong with me?' she asked indignantly, tucking her white cotton skirt loosely into the leg elastic of her briefs.

'You're a girl, miss,' said Billy, eyeing her tanned thighs in shock.

'Billy Love, you're growing up to be prejudiced. Look that up when you get home,' she scolded. 'I got a prize in climbing trees when I was at school. Besides, haven't you ever heard of Wonderwoman?'

With a grin at his doubtful face, she kicked off her shoes and made her way up. During her marriage to Sebastian she had occasionally evaded their invasive house guests for the peace and quiet of a treetop perch.

Getting up the tree to the kitten's refuge was no problem: getting it down was another matter. Eventually the spitting, snarling bundle of fluff calmed under her soothing voice, and Jade was able to lift it off the branch without too much bother. But she'd need both hands to clamber down. She undid the top button of her shirt and tucked the kitten firmly into the front of her dress, wondering what Billy would make of that!

With the furry ball snuggled against her breast, she had nearly reached the ground when an angry voice yelled at her.

'What the devil are you doing?'

Her fingers slipped in surprise and she only just managed to hang on, her startled heart thudding unnaturally in surprise. Then her mouth tightened and she continued on, wondering what Dane would make of her long, bare legs, her unbuttoned dress and the kitten jammed against her chest! She reached the lowest branch and swivelled around to jump, checking the distance to the ground.

Dane moved underneath her, just where she intended to land.

'Oh, do get out of my way,' she said in exasperation.

'Jump and I'll catch you,' he said, his face uplifted anxiously.

A vision of herself landing in his arms and being slid down his body flashed into her head.

'She doesn't need catching. She's got prizes in getting up trees,' said Billy, defending his idol.

'No one gets prizes for that,' he said, watching Jade like a hawk.

Jade glared. The bark on the tree was rough on her thighs and she wanted to jump.

'I won two packets of Smarties and admittance to Regent's Park Gang,' she yelled. 'I'd offer evidence, but I ate the Smarties and the gang has dispersed. They're probably all prizefighters now. Move away!'

With a resigned grin, he did so, folding his arms and straddling his legs ready to watch her descent as if he had paid to see a performance. Praying that she'd land gracefully, Jade slid off the branch and was briefly winded by the fall. She was heavier than she'd thought! Dane hadn't moved a muscle. She rose proudly.

'I thought you were in danger.' he said, capturing her eyes. 'I was all prepared to do my knight-in-shining-armour bit, and you adamantly refused to be a damsel in distress. Your behaviour is very unorthodox, Mrs Kendall.'

'You,' she remembered, 'nearly made me lose my grip up there . . .'

'Looking up at that expanse of leg made me lose my grip

down here,' he murmured.

Jade's face flamed. 'You'd better understand that I don't like people interfering in my life. If I want to climb trees, that's nothing to do with you. So, in future, make sure you mind your own damn business!' she finished with great satisfaction, marching off proudly.

'My cat!' wailed Billy.

She flushed and pulled the squirming bundle from her dress, aware that Dane was laughing at her.

With a deep breath of indignation, she marched off again.

'Your shoes!' came a chuckling male voice.

Infuriated, her eyes flashing sparks, high colour in her cheekbones, she took them from him and hurriedly pulled her skirt down.

'How about a truce?' he called after her retreating figure.

'I'm waiting!' she yelled back.

'What for?'

He'd make a lovely straight man, she thought in satisfaction. 'Hell to freeze over,' she cried, and was disconcerted by his roar of laughter.

CHAPTER FOUR

AFTER that, she didn't see him again, and that, of course, was exactly what she wanted. It irritated her, then, to find herself peering out of the window each morning to see if anyone was driving into the manor, and she'd turn at the sound of any vehicle in the village as she walked to and from school. It was difficult concentrating on her gardening too, because so many people were wandering around the grounds. She kept hearing voices—and kept listening for Dane's. It would have been better without Charlie's fence, then she could have given a quick glance and carried on, she thought glumly.

It really was silly, the way Dane occupied her thoughts so much. Perhaps when she got to know his wife it would be easier to think of him as a married man. He always seemed so *unmarried*; it was his attitude, of course.

Her own love-life wasn't going too well. Her relationship with Charlie had foundered; he'd actually given her up, saying that she was too unpredictable for him!

Gradually the upheaval next door died away, and it became obvious that the work must have been completed. The gossip was that Mr King was in New York, promoting one of his best-selling authors, yet someone had engaged two full-time gardeners and they were already working on the estate.

The school secretary returned, fully recovered from her illness, and with regret Jade left her job at the little school. Through it, she had not only occupied her mind successfully, but had also become properly integrated into the village at last. People trusted her.

Now Jade was left with time on her hands. Knowing she really ought to be working on her book, she rejected the idea because it was too lovely a day. Instead she picked flowers from her garden and took them to the little church. She was decorating the deep Norman window recesses happily, humming to herself, when a child's voice piped up. She didn't bother to look; visitors often came in to admire the church, and there had been six since she arrived. If she paid attention to them all, she'd never finish!

'Can I put them there? Can I really? Will Granny like that?' said the little boy anxiously.

'Granny will be delighted,' came Dane's gentle voice.

Jade froze momentarily, and then continued to arrange lilac, its heavenly fragrance delighting her senses.

'My flowers aren't as big as that lady's flowers,' said the child tremulously.

Jade had to look. It was the little boy who'd been dandled on the rosy-cheeked woman's knee at the auction. He was clutching a bunch of cow parsley, buttercups and daisies in his chubby fist.

'Size isn't important,' said Dane, crouching beside the boy. 'You picked them for her. You chose the ones you liked best. That's very special, if they're picked with love.'

Jade felt a pricking in the back of her eyes as the little boy nodded wisely and laid the flowers on the hands of the stone effigy in the chancel.

'She's like Granny, isn't she? She's even got a scarf thing around her head. What does it say here?'

'It tells us who she was. Matilda, sixth baroness of Saxonbury. She lived in the Manor a long time ago.'

'Is Soniver a baroness now? Are you a baron?'

'No,' said Dane, his eyes on Jade, who was furiously pushing foxgloves into place.

'Can I go and look at the graves outside?' The little boy was tugging at Dane's sleeve.

'Of course. Stay in the churchyard, though. I'll be out in a moment.'

There was a long pause. Jade moved on to another window, wishing Dane didn't have the capacity to be so darned nice. It was an awful combination with wicked sensuality.

'Hello, Jade.'

'Hello.'

'You look well.'

'Me?' She forced a lively expression to her face and turned towards him. 'I feel fantastic.' Her eyes travelled up and down his plain black suit. 'My goodness,' she gabbled, trying to say something to take her mind off the hungry, brooding way he was looking at her. 'You'll have to get a new wardrobe if you're coming to live down here. Aren't you hot in that?'

'I've just been to a funeral,' he said quietly. 'The woman who bid for me at the auction. I'm looking after her grandson for the day till his mother is over it all. Any more gibes? Do you want to jump to any more conclusions?'

'Oh, God, I'm sorry!' she said contritely, her shoulders slumping. 'I have an awfully big mouth.'

'Yes,' he agreed, staring at it and confusing Jade even more.

'I really am sorry,' she repeated. 'She looked as if she was a kind lady.'

'She was a good friend.'

Dane's fingers idly travelled over the carved draperies of Matilda's effigy while Jade struggled to accept the fact that he counted an ordinary-looking granny as one of his friends. It didn't fit with her impression of him at all.

'I don't suppose you know anyone who could be my cook/housekeeper in her place, do you?' asked Dane. 'I'd prefer someone who lived in the village and came in on a daily basis. How about you?'

'Me?' she said faintly. 'No, thank you. I have no wish to be your servant.'

He scowled. 'It's a job, not a boot-licking exercise.'

Jade frowned. Why did he make her want to be rude all the time? She considered for a moment, trying to atone.

'Mrs Love might do it, she only works in the post office two days a week. Now Billy is getting older she has more time to herself—and she enjoys cooking.'

'Thank you. I'll ask her. I saw Polly in your front garden and we stopped to say hello. She seems to have recovered well.'

'Yes; apart from a slight limp if she has a very long walk, she's fine. I was grateful to you that day,' she said impulsively. 'I'm not sure how I would have coped without you.'

'I told you, I have a knight-and-damsel fixation. Not many dragons left now, so I have to make do with smaller problems. Still, there are compensations.'

She swallowed to disperse the dry feeling in her throat as his eyes softened. 'Compensations?' she asked, knowing she should have taken no notice of his obviously pointed remark.

'Absolutely. I don't get my eyebrows singed any longer,' he said, grinning.

Jade laughed in relief. 'You're determined not to be thanked properly, aren't you?' she said shrewdly. 'But, nevertheless, Polly and I appreciate what you did.'

'So I'm not all bad?'

'Not all,' she said grudgingly.

'Well, we have taken one giant step forwards, Jade,' he said, quiet and serious. 'I think I'd better see where the lad is. He loved his granny very much, and he might be crying and in need of a comforting arm.'

Dane was rather good at that, thought Jade wistfully.

'Poor little kiddie. He was so sweet about his flowers, wasn't he?' she said mistily, her mind dwelling on the way Dane had handled the boy's concern about the value of his small offering.

'I don't think I've met any woman who looks so untamed on the outside and is utterly tender-hearted on the inside,' he murmured.

Jade's heart lurched crazily. 'You obviously don't move in the right circles,' she said tartly, to cover her confusion.

'Maybe. No signs of total surrender to my charms, yet?' he asked lightly.

She smiled coolly. 'Last time I looked, hell was still firing on all cylinders.'

'I know,' he said quietly. 'I was there, too.'

Jade watched his retreating back thoughtfully. Dane King was an enigma. Sometimes he epitomised everything in a man that she despised. Sometimes he was too warm and human for her own good. And sometimes, like just now, he let her glimpse a side of him that gave another dimension to his complex character. What hell could a man as successful as Dane King have experienced? He had everything he wanted.

For two weeks, he had commuted to London, leaving at seven, just at the time that Jade walked Polly to the church green. Mrs Love was full of the fact that Soniver King had not yet taken up residence, and that they weren't intending to share the master bedroom. Apparently Soniver had been installed in the big bedroom which Jade and Sebastian had used as a guest-room, across the corridor.

Mrs Love was scandalised at the way modern couples carried on, but her admiration for Dane overcame her doubts about his marital arrangements. Jade secretly thought that Dane and Soniver had separate rooms because it was easier to cheat on each other that way. She had become very cynical about life in the fast lane, after meeting Sebastian's friends.

Then her worst fears were realised. One Friday night, she was walking back to Rose Cottage after bell-ringing practice. She always enjoyed the hour she spent hauling on the thick bellropes with Charlie and the farmer's two sons, listening to the glorious peal of bells ringing out across the still evening air.

The stillness was shattered rudely when the first of a number of expensive-looking cars swept past her and drove into the manor. A cold memory balled in her stomach. It was starting, then, she thought dully. The parties, the cruel infidelities . . .

Jade pretended not to hear the admiring comments thrown at her from the open-topped sports cars. These people were beneath contempt. She was just unlatching her front gate when a breathlessly husky voice accosted her.

'Hello! You're Jade, aren't you? I'm Soniver King.'

Jade turned reluctantly, and took the slender hand.

'Dane's terribly reticent about you. I keep pumping him, but he gets aerated and snaps nastily. That's highly significant,' bubbled Soniver.

'Really?' Jade eyed the stunning cream trouser suit and delicate green camisole top, and wished she was wearing something more fetching than faded jeans and an old gingham shirt.

'Absolutely,' grinned Soniver. 'So I'm naturally fascinated. Are you doing anything right at this moment?'

'No . . .' Darn it! Why did she tell the truth?

'Good! Hop in, we're having an impromptu party. I told Dane it was about time he invited some people and he said over his dead body and I said how about a little barbecue and he said very well.'

Soniver beamed at Jade after the enthusiastic words, and despite herself Jade had to smile. She could see that Dane didn't have everything his way with such a bombastic wife!

'No, thank you, I——'

'You must! Heavens, we have to invite you, you're our nearest neighbour. I hope we'll be good friends, Jade.'

Perplexed that she felt immensely drawn to Soniver, Jade frowned. 'I have to feed my dog, and then . . .'

'Oh right, I'll wait,' said Soniver happily.

'I'm afraid you don't understand,' said Jade sharply, seeing that she'd have to make matters clear. 'I don't want to get involved. I don't want to see the inside of Saxonbury Manor again, ever. Nor do I want to enter its grounds.'

She didn't add that she had no wish to see Dane King lording it in her old home, nor what chic London style had done to the interior. Mrs Love had said it was very posh, but she had spared her feelings and not gone into lengthy descriptions. Jade gave a brief nod at the astonished Soniver and hurried into the cottage.

Feeling shaky, she fed Polly and prepared some supper for herself, staying indoors so that she wouldn't hear any noise from next door. But it was too lovely an evening, and she felt resentful that she was being forced to spend it indoors. This sort of thing would happen often; she might as well get used to it and not let it spoil her life.

So she took her notepad and books outside, intending to sit on her lawn and do a little more research while Polly lolled heavily on her bare feet.

When her dog rose, her tail wagging madly, Jade turned expecting to see one of the villagers, calling in for some eggs or honey. Instead, Dane was standing by her well. If he'd come to persuade her to attend his wretched barbecue, he had another think coming, she thought irritably. Wild horses wouldn't drag her to a party at the manor.

'I—I came to apologise for Soniver,' he said warily.

'Does she know that?'

'Of course.'

He came to sit a little way from her on the grass. Polly clambered all over him. Jade noted that he looked quite different in a tatty blue T-shirt and jeans in a worse state of repair than hers.

He saw her glance and explained, 'My wood-chopping outfit. About Soniver . . .'

'I'm sorry, it was my fault,' she said, not wanting to hear him talk of his wife. 'But she was very insistent that I should come to your darn barbecue, and I had to tell her eventually why I didn't want to go.'

'No, it was *my* fault, which is why I'm apologising. I omitted to tell her you weren't ecstatic about my ownership of Saxonbury. At the auction she thought you recognised my name and were overcome with astonishment at my fame,' he said with a wry twist to his mouth. 'She's a little biased in my direction, you understand.'

'How dutiful.'

'Er . . . yes. Then she was immersed in admiring villagers and didn't surface for ages. She's a bit vague and she missed the undercurrent of hostility completely. I've now explained.'

'I see. Thank you.' Jade picked up her book pointedly.

'She thinks you can be won over, though,' he said quietly.

'Well, she doesn't know me very well, does she?' said Jade in a kindly tone.

'There's no reason why we should remain enemies.'

'When I dislike someone, it takes a great deal to make me change my opinion,' she said coldly.

'But you don't dislike me, Jade.' Dane's eyes melted into hers and she gulped.

'You just can't accept that any woman could ever find you selfish, shallow and worthless,' she grated. 'You arrogant man!'

He leaned towards her and she moved back in alarm.

'You're afraid of me,' he said softly. 'Afraid of my kisses.'

Terrified, she thought! 'I certainly am not!' she cried hotly.

'Prove it.'

She regarded him in scorn. 'I'm not falling for that one,' she said. 'Go away. Can't you see I'm trying to work?'

'*I'm* trying to work out an amicable arrangement between us,' he coaxed. 'Soniver wanted to bring over some hot dogs and a bucket of flowers as an apology. She never does things by halves. But I thought she might make matters worse, whereas I——'

'Whereas you have considerable expertise in handling women,' she snapped.

'You're very keen on finishing my sentences, and making sure that I never forget that remark,' he said ruefully.

'It was an extremely unpleasant remark to make,' she observed, intently studying the page in front of her and seeing nothing.

Dane sighed. 'I wish I could get through your antagonism. I wish I could loosen you up.'

Jade felt the fierce sensation of an electrifying charge pulsating from him. Unwillingly, she looked up from her book and trembled at the flame in his eyes and the predatory expression on his face. And his wife was only a few hundred yards away.

'My God!' she cried in disgust. 'The more I see you, the less I like you! Go back to your guests, Mr King. I'm sure you'll find willing women among them. I'm not one, that's for sure!'

Without a word, he put Polly aside and rose smoothly to his feet, contemplating the angrily quivering Jade for several seconds.

'For the moment I'll ease up. But it's a temporary respite. I have the house that I wanted,' he said huskily, 'and one day I intend to have you. Take that as a warning, Jade.'

'I take it as an insult and a threat!' she cried. 'You're nothing but a philanderer, and I despise you!'

'I'll prove otherwise,' he said quietly. 'I don't know why you have this impression of me, nor why you persist in denying your own destiny. Whether you like it or not, there is a powerful chemistry existing between us and it's making me restless. More than that, I'm hungry. Very hungry,' he added throatily, his eyes avidly raking her body. Jade felt her bones liquefy in the heat his gaze generated. 'When we meet under the right circumstances, you'll be unable to deny your need, Jade. As I will be unable to deny mine. It's a time I look forward to with mounting desire. Till then.'

He turned on his heel, leaving Jade confused by her feelings. Polly limped after him and she yelled at her, furious that her dog couldn't tell a first-class bastard when she met one.

Jade was unable to work. Dane had ruined the lovely evening, and, as the laughter of Soniver's barbecue reached her ears, she gathered her things with a sob and ran indoors to spend the rest of the evening curled up on the sofa, wishing she could love Charlie, wishing she didn't always fall for renegades.

That was a bad weekend for Jade. The merriment at the manor made her nerves jangle and she began to sleep badly, waking in a cold sweat. Her head was filled with images that she had once successfully crushed, and over and over again her thoughts raced to the way she'd felt when she'd heard of Sebastian's sudden death.

It had been a horrific moment, one which had shocked her deeply and made her realise just how much she had altered, how twisted her values had become. Over and over again she went through that day the last time they were together, reliving the distress and resenting Dane more and more because he was preventing her from making a new life for herself by reminding her of the past.

When the cars left early on the Monday morning, she breathed a sigh of relief and felt free to wander the Downs again, now she was unlikely to bump into any of Dane's friends. As the days went on, it became apparent that Soniver rarely stayed at the Manor, whereas Dane invariably returned there each night after work.

Rarely alone, though. Mrs Love whispered in hushed tones to Jade that numerous women visited him, and often stayed. Forcing herself to look up when cars went by, obviously bound for the manor, she saw that Mrs Love was right. Women were flocking to him in droves. It seemed he was promiscuous and insatiable, though his dreadful reputation was safe. Mrs Love enjoyed her well-paid job too much to gossip any further, and Jade refused to discuss him or his behaviour. It pained her too much. Because the manor was at the end of the village, no one else saw who went in or out, and so his extra-marital affairs were kept secret.

One morning, Jade had collected the weekly village newsletter and began her deliveries. Up to now she'd pushed a copy through the letterbox of the Manor and half run down the drive, as though Dane might pop out and accost her at any moment.

This time he was standing in the doorway, watching her as she strode with apparent nonchalance towards him.

Not deigning to greet him, she handed over the informative newsletter, hoping to make a quick exit.

'Can I advertise in this thing?' he asked, as she whirled on her heel to go.

'You?' Jade was surprised. Most of the adverts were for second-hand items, outgrown clothes or bicycles. 'I don't think anyone here would like your old suits,' she said calmly.

His mouth tightened. 'I have some stuff you left which I don't want,' he said. 'I've written it all down. Will you take the advert or not?'

'You have to pay in advance,' she said, intimating that he was not to be trusted.

Dane felt in his inside pocket and then followed Jade's stare. A diminutive blonde in a see-through négligéé had appeared just behind him. His eyes ran up and down the blonde, whose lashes fluttered alluringly. Jade was disgusted.

'Up so early, Dodo?' asked Dane, not at all embarrassed.

The man had no shame! But Jade knew that in her anger was disappointment at such blatant proof of his infidelity.

'It *is* ten o'clock,' she said sarcastically.

The blonde made no effort to cover herself up, but smiled sweetly at Jade.

'I had one hell of a night,' she said dramatically. 'And it's all your fault, you monster!' She grinned at Dane as if she didn't mind.

'I think you were delighted that I overcame your . . .'

'Excuse me if I butt in,' grated Jade. 'You can conduct your private affairs when I've gone. You had an advert for me.'

'I'm ravenous,' said Dodo, catching Dane's arm.

His eyebrows lifted. *'Again?'*

'For heaven's sake,' snapped Jade.

'Just a minute,' sighed Dane. 'Dodo, you go in. You'll unnerve the starlings dressed like that, to say nothing of me and Mrs Kendall. I won't be long and we'll do something about that hunger of yours.'

'Angel,' murmured Dodo, drifting away.

Jade was very angry. 'I want to talk to you,' she seethed.

Dane adopted a listening attitude and she bridled at his mockery.

'Don't let that kind of thing happen again,' she raged. 'Never!'

'You don't want me to conduct two conversation at once?' he asked innocently.

'You know what I'm talking about! Don't flaunt your fancy women and have intimate exchanges with them while I'm around!'

'Jealous?'

'No, damn you! I find the whole thing disgusting!' She was rigid with fury, her whole body taut.

'I suppose if I tell you she's not my—er—fancy woman, you wouldn't believe me?'

'Darn right I wouldn't,' she breathed.

'Why won't you give me the benefit of the doubt?' he frowned.

'Oh, come on, I wasn't born yesterday! What evidence do you expect me to discount? You fast-moving City types are all the same.'

'That's ridiculous. There are good and bad people everywhere, the countryside included. What exactly is this hang-up you have about people like me?'

Her face became haunted. 'I find glib, two-timing men utterly despicable,' she breathed.

'You ought to get to know me before you make rash accusations,' he said quietly. 'Who knows, I could grow on you.'

'That space is reserved,' she said frostily.

'What for, icicles?'

'Certainly not for a man who has dolly birds popping out of the woodwork!' she cried. 'Now give me that advert.'

As he handed it to her and sorted out the right money, she had the distinct impression that he was amused. But couldn't for the life of her understand why.

Most people would be highly embarrassed and ashamed to be caught out in adultery, she thought as she stormed around the rest of the village, delivering newsletters at a tremendous rate. Not so Dane King. It was probably something to be proud of in his circle. She wondered what the people of Saxonbury would make of his infidelity.

In fact, he was to make a move so popular with everyone that he would probably have been forgiven almost anything. Jade answered her door one morning to find Dane outside with a sheaf of papers in his hand.

'Yes?' she said ungraciously.

'I'd like to talk to you about Barlock's house,' he said evenly. 'I think it can be kept in the control of the village, and I need your advice.'

'Why me?' she asked.

'I figured that if you approved, then everyone else would,' he said drily.

'All right,' Her tone didn't betray the fact that her pulses were hammering away in her body at the sight of him. She sighed inwardly, recognising that for all his unpleasant life-style, she still found him unbearably attractive. Today he was dressed in a black T-shirt and black jeans. He looked tanned, glowing with health, as if he'd run all the way from the manor, and very, very masculine in the way his clothes hugged his muscled body. Jade showed him into the sitting-room and kept her eyes fixed on the papers in his hands.

'I heard through the grapevine that repairs to the house had drained the account and had a chat with the treasurer,' he said. 'They're in big trouble, as you probably know. Not only does the roof need re-thatching, but there's incipient damp rising and the ice-room is collapsing from the thud of feet over the lawn.'

'I know,' she sighed. 'When we spoke off the record to the National Trust, they were very doubtful about taking on the house at all. We were thinking of having some jumble sales or something similar to raise money.'

'This Garland Day. Will that raise much?'

Jade shook her head. 'Only enough to play for the ice-cellars to be restored, we reckon.'

'I thought as much. I propose to set up a trust fund and finance the house properly. Apart from myself, there are plenty of wealthy lovers of literature who'd contribute to it. What do you think?'

She was too astonished to answer for a moment. 'Why on earth would you do such a thing?' she asked slowly.

'Does that matter?'

'Yes, it does.'

He smiled gently. 'I like this village, Jade. I like the people and I care about preserving everything in it. Fortunately Barlock Weir was in my line of business, and I can pull a lot of strings to help out. Well, do you think the idea will be welcomed, or will I be looked upon as a nosy interloper in village affairs?'

'I should think you'll be welcomed with open arms,' she said wryly.

'Good. One more thing. John Pavey has asked me if I'd like to be a school governor. Again, I don't want people to think I'm pushing myself into village life. I know I can count on you to give me an honest opinion.'

John Pavey obviously didn't know the kind of man Dane King was, mused Jade. He'd be quite unsuitable.

'No one would see that as being pushy. But you wouldn't like the duties,' she said dismissively.

'Oh? Like what?' he asked, leaning forwards, and a little too close in the small room for Jade's liking.

'It's a serious business. You have to attend meetings and discuss school affairs and make decisions about maintenance and finance and . . .'

'What makes you think I can't cope with that, Jade?' he asked, his eyes twinkling.

'Oh, you could run the whole darn show standing on your head,' she said sharply. 'That's the trouble, you'd get bored . . .'

'I'm flattered you should care,' he laughed.

Jade flushed. 'I meant you're too flashy and high-powered for our school. And you wouldn't like visiting. You'd be expected to spend time in the school itself.'

'I'd like that,' he said quietly. 'I'm very fond of children.'

She looked up and saw he was sincere, and felt a rush of warmth towards him. Perhaps he was childless because Soniver was unable to become pregnant. He'd shown that he had empathy with children when he'd looked after his late cook's grandson that day.

'Perhaps I'm wrong about you,' she said reluctantly. 'About being a governor, I mean.'

'I'd enjoy it enormously,' he admitted. 'It would give me a chance to play in their sandpit—— I've admired and envied it ever since I first arrived.'

She burst into gales of laughter at the thought of Dane making sandcastles.

'I held a "Who can build the silliest sandcastle? competition," she said, giggling at the memory. 'The best bit was joining the children in jumping on the sandcastles at the end.'

'You like children too, I can see that,' he grinned. 'Are you from a large family?'

'No, I was the only one. But our house was always filled with people, adults and assorted children. I'm not sure where they all came from, or even if they knew my parents, but it was fun.'

'They don't sound as if they're your average run-of-the-mill parents. Are they artists?'

'Artistes, I suppose,' she said. 'Father was a clarinettist in the London Symphony Orchestra, and Mother was an opera singer. Life was lavish and very Bohemian, very casual. Mother created all the drama you can imagine: if there wasn't some crisis in the offing, then she invented one. That was her Italian temperament, you see, but she was incredibly loving and I adored all the extravagant emotion. My schoolfriends' parents were dull in comparison.'

'I bet. You talk of your parents in the past tense,' he probed gently.

Her lashes swept down to cover her eyes, and then she lifted them, trusting him not to mock her misty gaze. 'Yes. They died just over two years ago. I was devastated.'

'Two powerful and vital lives suddenly gone,' he said.

'Exactly that.' She'd known he'd understand. It had seemed doubly cruel when her parents had loved life so intensely.

'I wish I could have been around to help,' he said with sadness.

Jade's heart twisted in pain. She wished he wasn't such a Jekyll and Hyde character, and then she wouldn't alternately long for him and despise him.

'Sebastian was there,' she said in an unemotional tone. 'He helped.'

'Ah, yes. Sebastian.' Dane had clammed up, all the softness in his expression wiped away, and Jade knew she'd been right to remind him about marriage partners. 'Well, thanks for the advice and encouraging support,' he said brightly. 'I'll get going on the trust, and you can be sure that Barlock's house will remain in village hands. And don't be surprised if you catch a rather large-looking child playing on the climbing frame in Jubilee Field. Give him a kind word, because it'll be me.'

She dimpled at him and showed him out, even more disturbed than before. He really could be awfully charming and likeable when he tried! She supposed that was the sign of a consummately skilled seducer. Not too far in the future she would have to liaise with him over the Garland Day celebrations, and she was dreading that intimacy which came with working closely with someone. Last year when she'd been involved it had just been good fun; this year she could already predict the tense atmosphere which would exist between them. Her only hope was that maybe by then he would have tired of playing the country gentleman and would have escaped to the more sophisticated pleasures of the city.

She both yearned for and feared that day, but knew for a certainty that it must come.

CHAPTER FIVE

THERE were other village activities more pressing than the flower show. Jade's time had been taken up for the past few days with preparations for the barn dance. It was a casual affair, and she had decided to wear a white cotton dress with a scooped back and neck to show off the tan she'd acquired from working in the garden. Since she was going on her own, and wouldn't have to fend off an escort, she felt free to wear whatever she liked, and she knew she was looking good that evening.

With a group of friends, she made her way down the cart track to the big barn, owned by the local farmer. It had been decorated inside with streamers and balloons, and looked very festive. Down one side were trestle-tables groaning with food. Jade was grabbed for a dance the minute she walked in. One of the farmer's sons whirled her around in an exuberant reel, bringing the colour to her cheeks and a sparkle to her eyes.

When the dance finished and the fiddler paused for a drink, she saw that Soniver and Dane had arrived and were chatting with the vicar. Soniver was breathtakingly lovely, even in white stretch jeans and a skimpy yellow top. Jade's reluctant eyes flickered to Dane, admiring his brown suede trousers and short-sleeved cream shirt, open at the neck. He looked very virile and powerful, dominating the company with a naturally commanding presence. Soniver kicked her shoes off and pulled him on to the dance-floor.

'Hello, Jade!' she yelled as she was whisked past.

Jade smiled briefly in her direction. There was no doubt, she thought, as the evening wore on, that Soniver King could charm birds off trees. No wonder she'd snared Dane. Soniver had danced with every man there, and somehow managed not to antagonise any wives. Jade was full of admiration, and sat at the plank bar watching Soniver dancing with Charlie, who was loving every bit of the 'Boomps-a-Daisy'. The music finished and Dane appeared at her side.

'I think,' he said, sitting on the hay bale next to her, 'that people will talk if we don't dance together.'

'I think they'll talk if we do,' she said calmly, despite her thudding heart. Tonight there was a very slow sensuality about him; either he was drunk or aroused by the antics of his wife, and she had no intention of touring the floor in his arms with him in that kind of mood.

'Dane!' Soniver grabbed his arm urgently. 'I had no idea how late it was! I've had a wonderful time. I was only going to stay for an hour and a half, but I really must go. I've got to get up at four-thirty, remember.'

'Damn!'

He flicked a glance at Jade and then back at his wife. Foiled again! thought Jade triumphantly.

But she was wrong. Soniver was generous to a fault. 'You stay, darling. Charlie's going to walk me to my car and then he'll come back again. I can sort out the details of that fireback that he's going to make for us on the way.'

'You're driving up to London?'

'I'd rather stay in the flat tonight, darling. I can catch a couple of hours' sleep before I dash off to Toyko.'

'All right. Watch out for that Charlie in the dark out there. He bumped bottoms with a little too much enthusiasm.'

'You're so protective!' she grinned, kissing his cheek and giving him a hug. 'Bye, darling. Bye, Jade. Perhaps I ought to warn her about you,' she said saucily.

'No need,' he said with an easy grin. 'She's impervious to my immense charm.'

'Bored rigid by its insincerity,' corrected Jade with a sweet smile.

Soniver grinned. 'Oh, Dane! It looks as if she's got your measure! No wonder you find her fascinating.'

Ignoring Jade's wide-eyed astonishment, Soniver drifted off to find her shoes, and it was several minutes before she finally left. By that time the accordionist and fiddler were playing something dreamy and the lights had dimmed, to squeals of delight from the teenagers. Dane's hands lifted Jade off the hay bale as she was still trying to come to terms with Soniver's remarks. Was that why Dane pursued her—because she didn't leap into bed with him? If so, it might be more difficult to get rid of him than she had thought, since the only way to make him lose interest was to surrender!

Suddenly she discovered she was stupidly standing in the circle of his arms, and he was watching the fleeting expressions on her face with lazy amusement. With a quick intake of breath, she tried to escape.

'Don't struggle,' he murmured in her ear. 'People near us are watching.'

He threw her a crooked smile and drew closer, moving with her on to the dance-floor. Jade felt a quiver run down her spine as his hand slipped around to splay warmly over her bare skin. She held herself very erect, wishing he'd do more than sway sensually to the music and look at her with bedroom eyes. All kinds of sensations were chasing through her body, creating needs she had long forgotten.

'Jade,' he murmured, bringing her head to rest against

his chest. She made to move back, but his arm was like a steel band. Gradually she became aware of the heat of his body and the way his fingers burned into her flesh. He was tense with desire, a wayward pulse leaping in his jaw, the hard thrust of his hips telling her that he was highly aroused and determined to let her know this fact.

Gritting her teeth, she tried not be affected by him, but he was a master of seduction. The way he breathed, the way he shifted his body, the way he looked at her with such depth of meaning—all combined to form an irresistible and potent sexual lure.

Jade's head spun as the flames of passion rose within her. Whatever attraction this man possessed, she seemed helpless in its path.

'I want you,' he murmured.

A stab of desire shot through Jade's body, and she was ashamed. 'I'm well aware of that,' she said coldly. 'And probably half the village is aware of it, too. Have you no control?'

'None. And you're fast losing yours, Jade—don't pretend otherwise. Ever since we first set eyes on one another it's been obvious that we'd end up together.' His fingers surreptitiously massaged the back of her neck.

'Has it, indeed?' she said in a ridiculously high voice, crushing the electrifying sensation his touch produced. 'You're tickling. Stop it.'

'No, I'm not. You're loving it. Jade! I want to kiss you very badly!'

Shocked by his intensity, she slanted her eyes at his mouth and instantly regretted it, watching his lips part hungrily. Her breath became erratic and her legs so shaky that she knew she couldn't move away or she'd make a fool of herself and stagger from the wonderful, hazy weakness.

Everyone would know that she'd been rendered helpless by Saxonbury's untamed Don Juan. And yet, if she stayed in his arms, he'd continue to seduce her! The dilemma was intolerable.

'I wish you'd leave me alone,' she mumbled miserably.

'Not till I have what I want,' he whispered in her ear.

His warm breath sent shivers down her neck. 'Please, Dane . . .'

'Yes. I intend to,' he promised huskily.

Jade's eyes closed. What she felt right now was indecent. He was married! Her panic-stricken eyes flickered to the door. It was near. Suddenly she ducked out of his arms and ran out, not caring what anyone thought. She'd long earned a reputation for behaving in an odd way, and the villagers wouldn't find anything surprising in her actions tonight with any luck. To her dismay, as she stumbled down the cart track in the semi-darkness, she heard Dane calling out to her.

With a muttered exclamation, she slipped over the low wall into the school playground, but he'd seen her and vaulted the wall in one easy leap.

'Jade!'

A moan escaped her lips. She made a frantic dash to Jubilee Meadow, too afraid of her own responses even to face him in anger. It was there that he caught her up. An arm suddenly snaked around her waist and she was being hauled roughly back against the length of his hard, virile body. For a moment, she tried to catch her breath, and that gave him boldness. His right hand crept teasingly towards her heaving breast while she struggled unsuccessfully to speak; petrified with fear, trembling with unwanted desire.

One long forefinger lightly touched her nipple and it rose treacherously to a hard peak. Dane groaned and bent his head to kiss her neck, his finger creating more pleasure with its tiny, circular movements than she'd every experienced before. This was madness! Jade was still paralysed, wanting his touch to go on, hating herself utterly.

She let out a breath and threw back her head, the long black hair falling like a waterfall.

'*No!*'

'*Yes!* You've driven me crazy over the last few months. I know how badly you want me, every part of your body tells me. I'd be mad to let you go now. This lovely summer evening, Jade, this black night, in this sweet meadow; here is the place I will make love to you!'

Her breast was swollen and engorged. She had to bite her lips to prevent herself from demanding that he must arouse the other one too.

'No, Dane,' she said miserably. 'You mustn't! Your wife . . .'

'Mmm?' he muttered, only half listening, his teeth nibbling her shoulder.

'Your *wife!*'

He turned her around to face him. 'What on earth has she got to do with us?' he asked, astonished.

Jade went cold with horror. 'You bastard!' she breathed. 'The minute she leaves you, you make a play for me——'

'Wait a minute,' he laughed. 'It was all of five years ago that she left me. That's hardly rushing things.'

Her perplexed face made him look at her more carefully. 'I'm divorced, Jade,' he said quietly. 'Not very amicably, but everyone has to go through hell once in their lifetime, I suppose.'

Hell? That must be what he'd been talking about . . . Jade shook her head to clear it.

'But Soniver—who is she, then? Your mistress?'

'Surely you know she's my sister?' he said in amazement, sighing when she stared uncomprehendingly at him. 'That wretched woman! It never occurs to her to introduce herself in a civilised way. Scatterbrain that she is!'

'She's got red hair!'

'Good lord, no one has real hair that colour! She's dark, like me.'

'It looks real,' she said doggedly.

'Yes, well she can afford to have it done expertly. She's in a highly paid job—I ought to know, I employ her and I pay her. She's on my staff and runs my New York office. Dammit all, did you really think I'd wave goodbye to a wife and try to seduce you all in the space of half an hour?'

'Yes.'

'Thanks. You have a pretty poor opinon of me, I see.'

Jade nodded. She had.

'How long have you been under the impression I was married?' he asked softly.

'Since we met,' she said nervously.

'Now I understand! How very satisfying. That explains everything.' His smile was dangerous. Jade had the sensation that she was in deep trouble now.

'No, it doesn't,' she said quickly, moving back and being swung into his arms again. 'I'll—I'll——'

'Scream?' he murmured. 'Haven't we done that one before? It was enjoyable, but I like variety. How about . . .' His melting eyes contemplated her mouth. 'I know. We could play guessing games.'

'Guess . . .' Her voice tailed away into thin air.

'Yes, you shut your eyes and guess where I'm going to touch you next, and if you get it wrong, I kiss you.'

'What . . .' Jade cleared her choked throat. She was going to regret asking this. 'What if I get it right?' she breathed.

'Oh, then I kiss you, of course,' he smiled.

'Oh.' She frowned. There was something wrong with that, though she was too confused to work out what it was exactly. Her brain seemed focused on the way his fingers were exploring the contours of her naked back. 'I don't want to play any games. I want . . .'

'Me,' he growled throatily.

'Dane . . .'

'Sweet Jade, you can't carry a torch for your late husband for ever,' he said gently. 'You are young and beautiful and in need of loving. Here I am, here you are and here is this lush grass waiting for our bodies. Forget the man you married. You can't stay faithful to his memory all your life. I'm here, real, alive and needing you. Let me help you to forget him.'

Forget! If only she could! Jade moaned softly. If only she hadn't visualised the terrible moment when she came across Sebastian and his secretary, naked, making love in the grass that day!

She had become deathly still and his last, desperately spoken words reflected his realisation that he had lost her. He stared in frustration at the blank eyes which were filled with pain. His hands dropped away and he dug his nails into his palms.

It was several seconds before he had controlled himself sufficiently to speak. Jade was still numb and cold, hardly breathing, trying to shut Sebastian out of her mind.

'I said the wrong thing. I don't usually make mistakes like that and I'm sorry. I had no idea you were grieving so much. He must have been one hell of a man. I'll see you home,' he rasped.

Wordlessly she walked beside him, as silent and passionless as a zombie. At her front door, he reached out and tentatively touched her hair.

'I'm worried about you. Will you be all right?'

'You have to leave me alone,' she said tonelessly. 'If you like me at all, do that. I can't bear what's happening to me. You make me upset.'

'I realise that now. I'll try,' he whispered. 'God knows, I'll try.'

In the same mesmerised daze, Jade walked into the cottage and straight up to her bedroom. Carefully she undressed, stepped into the shower and soaped herself with infinite care before letting cold water flood over her pinkened body.

Then she curled up in bed and lay very still, not moving, not thinking. Providing she didn't think, she told herself, the anguish wouldn't surface. One barrier to wanting Dane had been removed, and it would be harder to resist him, but she couldn't get involved with someone who would hurt her as badly as she'd been hurt before.

It seemed that Jade had only just fallen asleep when the telephone rang. Groggily she sat up in bed and stumbled downstairs in her short cotton nightdress, seeing to her astonishment that it was morning.

'Jade?'

'Damn you, Dane!' she raged in sudden, inexplicable fury. 'I told you . . .'

'You said keep away and I'm doing that. I had to ring this morning to find out if everything was all right. I've hardly slept at all, wondering. I nearly came to see you. This is very restrained of me, you know.'

'What time is it?' she muttered.

'Eight o'clock and I'm late for work. I've been ringing for the last hour and I've been going frantic. Tell me how you are and I'll ring off.'

'Tired.'

He swore. Then spoke more gently. 'Go back to bed, Jade. I'm sorry I woke you. I had to ring.'

In the days following after that, he did ring occasionally with a polite enquiry, and she would tell him she was fine. In fact, she was feeling increasingly lonely and knew that she missed him. When three weeks had passed he called in one evening on his way home from work while she was listlessly eating supper in the garden, her books spread around her.

Polly was ecstatic, of course.

Jade looked longingly at the elegant figure in the silver-grey summer suit. He was hugging the retriever affectionately and a lump formed in her throat. His features seemed intensified by his absence, his brow smoother, his cheekbones higher, his mouth and eyes filled with more desire than she'd ever seen them. But his tone was properly distant. If it hadn't been, she might have run to him and let herself be swept into his immoral world for a short while.

'I heard you had some honey for sale.'

'Honey and eggs,' she said brightly.

'I'd like some, please.'

'Step this way, sir,' she called gaily, dropping him a mock curtsey and leading him into her kitchen.

Her fumbling fingers selected the eggs from the big basket and put them into the egg box.

'Laid this morning,' she said 'They're still warm. I expect those two will have double yolks—they're big enough. They tend to topple out of egg cups, though,' she babbled on wildly. 'That's why I can't sell them through the normal channels. My hens lay funny-shaped eggs.'

'They would,' he said drily.

'Yes,' she said with a nervous laugh. 'It must be

something to do with the things I tell them.'

'Pardon?'

'When I talk to the bees—you *must* know you have to tell bees what goes on—I think the hens hear, too. They always cluster around my feet hopefully, thinking it's feeding time. Anyway——' Jade was conscious of the fact that she had launched on a long, inconsequential speech and didn't know how to finish. Her fingers twisted. 'Well, they do tend to go broody after that and lay enormous eggs.

'I see.' Dane's eyes studied her seriously.

Jade fiddled with the box. 'Is a dozen enough?'

'Thank you. And two jars of honey, please.'

They both knew that Mrs Love did the shopping for him. Buying eggs and honey was an excuse. Jade didn't want to spoil the charade: she was seeing him and talking to him, and for the moment that was enough. Dane King was like a drug that she couldn't give up.

As he dropped the money into her open palm, he hesitated. 'How's the situation in hell?' he asked.

'Still not frozen,' she said quietly, her lashes lowered.

'I see. Er . . . next week . . . I expect I'll be needing some more eggs and honey.'

'Yes. Fine. See you then.'

So every week, apart from the chance meetings in the village or on the Downs when they both greeted each other briefly and went on their way, they went through the same ritual. Always he wanted to know whether hell had frozen over, and she told him it hadn't.

That was a barren time for Jade, lit by the brief moment when he stood in her kitchen—moments which were followed by self-recrimination and emptiness. Perhaps the only one good thing to come out of the empty weeks was that she had made a great deal of headway on the history of Saxonbury village and its surrounding area. Soon, though, she would be hampered by the fact that the books she needed were in the manor library, and she didn't want to ask if she could research there, not with different women coming and going on days he stayed at home. His promiscuity was bad enough without witnessing it in close-up.

One Friday she heard his car drawing up outside as usual, a little late. She'd been waiting nervously, unable to settle, listening for the familiar throaty roar, and was relieved when it eventually arrived. But this time there was a woman in the passenger seat and it wasn't Soniver.

Jade's eyes glazed with pain. He was obviously trying to tell her something, to show her that he'd waited long enough and there were other fish in the sea. Miserably she stared through the window at the woman. She was about thirty, tiny, fragile and with long, straight, brown hair. She wore no make-up and had an interesting, arresting face: a woman of character. Jade would have preferred her to be a glamorous blonde. This one was the kind who could hold a man by personality alone.

Glumly Jade went through the ritual of selling him produce he didn't need to buy, and suddenly could bear it no longer. As Dane made to leave, and join his companion, she came to a decision.

'Wait, Dane. I have an idea,' she said, keeping her head down and taking a long time to put the money away in her purse. 'Why don't I get Mrs Love to pick up what eggs and honey you need? She passes by here most mornings, and it would save you calling in on your way home. You must be tired after a day's work. It does seem silly for you to do the shopping, doesn't it?'

He turned his back on her, the broad shoulders masking

any reaction as he stood looking down her garden. Anxious to remember as much detail of him as possible, she devoured everything about him: that neat dividing line of black hair and tanned neck, the intricate folds of his ears, the set of his shoulders and the width of his back. Then he spoke quietly.

'I wonder why neither of us thought of that before?'

'One never sees the obvious,' she said with a nervous laugh, her eyes continuing their wistful journey over his body.

He spun around. 'No. Perhaps you're right. And one thing is obvious, Jade,' he said, his voice growing harsh, his face taking on a cruel expression. 'You are married to a dead man!'

Jade flinched at the pain within her. He didn't know how that hurt her! If only she could tell him—but then he'd be relentless in his pursuit of her.

'Don't keep your woman-friend waiting,' she spat.

'Jade, she——'

'I don't want to hear! You are hurting me more than you can know! Go and look after her, she looks as if she needs your comfort . . .'

'She does, she——'

Jade's curse shocked them both. Dane hesitated for a moment and then, with an angry snarl, banged the egg boxes and the jars of honey down on her kitchen table.

'I have my pride,' he growled. 'I'm tired of being scorned and sworn at, of being reviled and told I can't be trusted! Lie in your damn lonely bed, Jade, and warm yourself with memories if you want—I need a flesh and blood woman, not one who lives in the past, however tempting she might be!'

Jade picked out one of the eggs and threw it wildly at

him, missing completely. With a snort of derision, he stormed out of the cottage.

Jade's anger and bitterness at Dane's cruelty succeeded in turning her against him, and she renewed her life with a determined vigour, entering enthusiastically—if a little wildly—into everything: the Lewes May Revels, the Raft Race down the Ouse River, the Beacon Bonfire party on Midsummer's Day when fires were lit on ancient beacon sites in an unbroken link across Sussex.

To the last event, Dane brought his tiny companion, setting alight the local gossip. The villagers knew by now that Soniver was his sister, and had apparently learnt from one of the gardeners that the woman he acted so protectively towards had been staying in the manor with him for some weeks now.

Jade laughed and sparkled brilliantly that evening as the wine flowed and the fireworks broke overhead. Dane kept back from the general merriment, preferring to look on. It was Jade who led everyone in a dance around Saxonbury Hill's ancient fortifications, each person holding a blazing torch. It was Jade who regaled the children with stories and legends from the past, imbuing them with dramatic excitement, sending thrills into her listeners as she spoke in hushed tones of witchcraft and magic, of local battles and the Great Plague which left the village decimated and filled the churchyard.

And all the time, surrounded by fascinated children and their parents, she was conscious only of one man and his woman.

Dane stood against the skyline just above Jade, silhouetted in the red blaze of the beacon fire, his arm around the woman. That could have been her, Jade thought, though she doubted she would have kept his interest very long. From under her lashes, she noted he looked deeply intent, as if he was listening to every word she said—the woman, too. Her heart ached to see them together so publicly. She refused to think of what they got up to in private. Her early instincts had obviously been right: the fragile, interesting woman was able to hold Dane's interest and fulfil his sexual needs.

At the stroke of midnight, Charlie rang the biggest bell in the church, far below. The last note died away and every-one was silent, watching the beacons flicker on distant hills as they had for centuries. Helpless to prevent herself, she lifted her lashes and stared at Dane. His eyes glittered red in the light and his dark figure looked threatening. Then he turned pointedly to his companion and blocked Jade out.

Filled with a sudden energy that had to be set free, she jumped up and organised a version of the Garland Dance, all the way down the hill and back to the village hall where hot soup was waiting for them. As she laughed and chatted, teased and exuded vitality, the image of Dane, almost supernaturally sinister, filled her head like a recurring nightmare.

Shivering with the intensity of the image, she vowed to be careful. It had almost seemed as if he had been trying to dominate her mind with his, taking advantage of the heightened tension of that night to catch her unawares. He was a dangerous, determined man, but she was strong now: he must have seen how cheerful she was, how she had driven away any residual need of him.

It wasn't long before her new strength would be put to the test. On the following Saturday morning, she blithely picked up the telephone to hear his voice and she was immediately on her guard.

'There's a swarm of bees hanging from one of my chestnut trees,' he began curtly, without any greeting or preamble. 'Anything to do with you?'

'Darn! I'll find out. Wait a moment.' Hot from her dash down to the end of the garden, which confirmed that they were hers, she counted up to twenty before picking up the phone again. 'Yes. I'll come over. Don't do anything, you could upset them.'

'I hadn't quite thought of it like that,' he said drily.

'Well, do,' she said sharply. 'There's a thunderstorm in the air and they'll be enraged.'

She cut off his question by putting the phone down, angry with herself. Earlier that morning she'd thought the hive was unusually excited, and just put it down to the brewing summer storm, which always disturbed them. Instead, a new queen had emerged and flown off with some of the drones to find a new nest.

Darn! She didn't relish tramping into the manor in her beekeeper's outfit, but there wasn't any alternative. She hurriedly stuffed everything she would need into a large wicker basket and set off, forcing a bright expression on to her face.

At least he had managed to prise himself away from his woman, she thought sourly to herself, as she saw him waiting for her alone at the top of the drive in his old jeans and top. He came forward to help carry her gear.

'Sorry about this. I hope you're not going to sue them and me for trespass. I couldn't hope to pay the fines of a few hundred sexless creatures,' she joked.

'Just get rid of them,' he said curtly.

'Show me where they are, then.'

'Down here. What was that you were saying about a

thunderstorm?' he asked as they walked across the immaculate green lawn. Jade was trying not to notice how lovely the grounds looked and how much work had been done to improve them.

'Any change in the electrical field sends them crazy,' she said. 'I can usually tell when a storm is brewing long before it's apparent in the sky by the way they buzz. They react to negative charges too, which is why people talk to them, especially if someone dies.'

Her voice shook as she said that and she bit her lip, remembering how she had run full tilt down the garden to sit by the hive when Sebastian had died. His two friends, who had come to tell her, thought she was mad. But it was tradition. A silly superstition. One that brought her some kind of comfort, sitting there in the meadow, trying to gain control of her emotions.

'There they are,' Dane's tone had grown harsher. It seemed he saw the invasion of her bees as an infringement of his privacy. 'Do you need any assistance, or would you prefer to do this on your own?'

'I don't need anyone,' she said, tossing her head.

'Really?'

He turned on his heel and strode towards the terrace where he had been drinking morning coffee. Jade donned her protective clothing, pulled the veil over her face and gently puffed smoke at the swarm, which was hanging like a living bag from the big branch. Then began the delicate task of slipping the swarm into her sack. When she'd finished she packed up her things and, in straightening up, directly faced the terrace.

Dane was embracing his woman, his arms wrapped tenderly around her. She was only wearing a cotton dressing-gown and, as her head was on his shoulder and she was clutched tightly to him, he must have felt every curve of her body.

The knives of cruel jealously tore into Jade relentlessly. Now she knew for sure. His supposed passionate desire for her had been easily satisfied elsewhere—whereas hers would never even know fulfilment. Hot, stinging tears sprang to her eyes and she cursed her emotional nature soundly.

Seeing them together like that had been the final straw. She fixed the sack on to a shoulder pole and moved quietly away so they didn't see her. It did hurt, there was no point in denying that. What she had to do was to get over him somehow. Once she was out of sight, she let free the sobs which had been held back, hurrying blindly down the lane and hoping no one would see her. But she bumped into Charlie.

'Here, you're too little to be carrying that lot,' he said in his slow voice. 'And what's upset you?'

He shouldered all her burdens and Jade wanted suddenly to let him take another one. 'Oh, Charlie!' she wailed.

'Here, don't carry on like that. Are these your bees in here?'

She nodded, sobbing.

'Go indoors. I'll get them sorted,' he said.

'They're angry . . .'

'I know that,' he said impatiently, giving her a push. 'Go on. Make some coffee or something. Shan't be long.'

They sat down together at the kitchen table and he listened patiently while she told him how she had been unwillingly attracted by Dane King and that he had pursued her for a while, until he'd found solace in another woman's arms.

'The devil! Want me to thump him?' asked Charlie.

She smiled weakly. 'No. I feel such a fool, Charlie, being interested in such a cad.'

'Forget him, he's not worth you. You're too good for him. To be honest, Jade when you and Sebastian first came here we all thought you were both fast. Slick, townie-like. Now I know you're different. Funny how you get the wrong impression of people, isn't it?'

'I made a mistake finding something to like about Dane King,' she said bitterly.

'Well, that's over now, isn't it?' he said cheerfully. 'You can't fancy a man who changes his sheets so often.'

Jade laughed through her tears. 'No,' she agreed. He'd put it very well. 'I can't.'

He stayed and chatted till it became clear that the storm would soon break and he had to hurry home. Jade sat in the unnaturally darkened room and thought. Being able to share her secret with Charlie had helped enormously.

There had been something naïvely stubborn in the way that, deep down, she had kidded herself Dane wasn't really corrupt and that the women who had visited were good friends. Of course he'd slept with them. He evidently enjoyed women—and he said himself that he liked variety. Jade wasn't making that mistake again. The manor seemed to attract bastards. The storm broke with savage ferocity, the lightning searing the room with blinding flashes. When it died away, Jade felt that the air had cleared and the rain had washed away all her earlier innocent stupidity.

CHAPTER SIX

WITH a deep sigh of contentment, Jade leaned back against the massive trunk of the ancient oak. There was something very comforting and strengthening about its permanence. It had probably been there when soldiers of King Henry the Eighth had ridden to nearby Lewes and blown up the great Priory, which dominated the countryside for miles around. It would have been there when the excise men hanged Jack Carter on the village green, for indulging in the local pastime of smuggling. In this valley, designated an area of outstanding natural beauty and therefore protected by the law, the oak would probably stand for at least two more centuries before it began to decay. Sussex people might come and go, love, hate, cry or laugh, but the countryside shed its magic regardless, answerable only to the seasons and defying man's puny efforts to destroy it.

Sitting here, or in the branches of the oak, had always put a different perspective on Jade's troubles. Life was meant for living and looking ahead, not for wistful thinking. And it was here that she came to persuade herself that Dane King meant nothing to her, nothing at all.

She had reached a stage in her writing where she could no longer continue without referring to the books in the manor. Knowing she needed a little time to consider the best way to approach Dane, she was using that time profitably by sketching features she wanted to include in her book.

So she sat working, with the clear sky overhead and

a slight breeze wafting the scent of wild honeysuckle towards her. The view across the Ouse valley was superlative; the groves in the skyline on Mount Caburn indicating clearly its ancient ditch and ramparts; the foreground taken up with interlacing brooks.

It was mid-morning and a few hikers had walked past, stopping to chat and admire her sketch, otherwise she was alone—if you didn't count the birds who were filling the air with a torrent of song.

Polly's tail began to wag and then she quietly left her position just behind Jade and went to welcome the man who appeared out of the wood. Engrossed in sketching, Jade didn't notice and the man didn't disturb her, but sat a few feet above and watched intently.

She froze, her pencil held in mid-air. A kingfisher sat on a nearby branch, its elongated head craning over the brook. Then, in a brilliant streak of iridescent turquoise, it had dived and returned with a small silver minnow wriggling in its beak. Jade was amazed at Polly's self-control, but didn't dare to turn and see why she was so quiet, till the kingfisher flew off, startled by a shout from a distant walker.

And as she turned her neck prickled, knowing someone was there, so she was half-prepared for the sight of Dane, sitting with one hand over Polly's muzzle, the other on her back holding her down.

'Oh, it's you. I wondered why she wasn't whining with frustrated excitement,' said Jade casually as Dane released the retriever and came down to sit beside her.

'I used to watch kingfishers on my father's farm. We had dogs, too, and they always appeared at the wrong moment,' he explained.

'Farm? *You* are the son of a farmer?'

He laughed at the look on her face. 'I certainly am.

You look shocked. My family have farmed for the last few hundred years.'

'But not you.' He wasn't the type, of course, she thought.

'My father sold up and went to live in the Algarve for health reasons,' he said quietly. 'I go and visit them as often as I can and take back-numbers of *Farmer's World*. I'm steeped in the life—that's why I love it here. I have the best of both worlds. The excitement and pace of London, its concerts and exhibitions, the immediate feed-back from publishers, and the peace and quiet, the closeness with my roots.'

'You feel like that?' She could hardly credit it. If ever a man had a split personally, it was Dane King!

'Very deeply,' he said, watching her carefully. 'I think I have the same reaction to this beautiful countryside as you.'

'Oh!' Jade struggled with the temptation to give in to her instincts to like him. He was beginning to sound too much like the sort of man who would suit her, but he was morally flawed.

She returned to her sketch, knowing that she was making unnecessary marks on the paper.

'I actually came looking for you,' he said. 'This wasn't an accidental meeting. Billy said he thought you were somewhere on this patch.'

Making a mental note to glare at Billy next time she saw him, she let her irritation show.

'Well, you've found me. What is it?'

'I had a phone call about the marquee you ordered for the Garland Day. There seems to be a problem. They rang the manor because that's apparently where all the arrangements are normally made from.'

It was what Jade had feared; she couldn't put off involving Dane any longer.

'Oh, dear. Yes, I should have done something about that. Whoever owns the manor plays a leading part in all of the organisation.'

'Thanks for telling me,' she said sarcastically.

'You're welcome.'

'Are you also going to tell me what I have to do, or by being Lord of the Manor is there some kind of Divine Inspiration?' he asked testily.

Abandoning her sketch, she tucked her knees under the golden print skirt and hugged them to her chest. Perhaps she could persuade someone else to attend their preliminary meetings, too.

'We have to get together for some of the arrangements. The idea is that I am to guide you through this year's events and you run it next year.'

'Hell!' His hand thrust impatiently through his hair, making black curls drop on to his forehead, just like the day she first saw him. A pang went through Jade.

'No, I'm not too keen on the idea either, but I'm sure we can manage to be civilised about it all for the sake of the village,' she said quietly.

'Yes, I suppose so. Isn't it a bit late to be starting now?'

'I've already made the major bookings,' she said, a little shame-faced. 'I didn't want to involve you at that stage.'

'I see. But . . . I'll have to fit our meetings in with my work. After dinner would suit me best.'

'Oh! I thought we'd sort things out in my house,' said Jade, disliking his suggestion. She wanted to be on her own home ground.

'On my land, on my terms, or not at all,' he said curtly. 'I have to be on call, near my own phone.'

'After dinner?' Her brows rose in query. 'No one's going to ring you then.'

'I run an international organisation. Problems come in at all hours of the day or night.'

'That must be inconvenient at times,' murmured Jade.

He shot her a suspicious glance. 'It is. And while we're on the subject, you might tell me what I can do about the fantails. They wake us up at the crack of dawn, tapping their beaks on the window.'

Jade laughed, imagining the scenario and how his woman must hate being woken. That must interfere with his early morning antics!

'Try a banquet,' she said callously.

'What?' He frowned. 'You mean send them invitations?' he asked with heavy sarcasm.

'No. Serve them up as dish of the day.'

Dane seemed to be considering the idea seriously, and a flicker of alarm went through Jade's head. He could be irritated enough with having his sleep disturbed. Or maybe he had been in the middle . . . She bit her lip and passed that one by, but not before thinking of his potential wrath if his smooth technique was ruined! He might kill off the birds in revenge!

'I could hold a medieval pageant,' he said slowly, seeing the possibilities. 'With a theme. That would mean bird's nest soup as a starter. Any ideas for pudding?'

'You're kidding,' she accused, deciding not to suggest chocolate eggs. He looked rather forbidding suddenly.

'Yes. I am. Now how about some sensible help?' he said tightly.

'Go to bed earlier and get up when they do.'

'No point in the former,' he growled. 'I spend half the night awake as it is. And I'm damned if I'm getting up at five-thirty!'

Angrily disturbed by visions of him and his live-in

lover writhing naked in her big four-poster, Jade found that her composure was cracking. Her body had tensed at his words, and she made a conscious effort to relax all her muscles.

'Are they hatching eggs?' she asked.

'Yes. Do you think I'm not feeding them enough?'

'It's not that. One bird will be sitting on the nest and might not be around at feeding time. Or you could be losing grain to the sparrows and so on. It's the cock birds who'll be hungry because they do the day shift.'

'You're joking!' he cried. 'I had no idea pigeons were involved in demarcation rules.'

Jade smiled faintly. 'I suggest you throw out more food in the meantime and get yourself a permanent food hooper.'

'Thank you,' he said gratefully. 'I'll try that. What about this marquee?'

'Oh, heavens! I'd forgotten that! It's vital. If there's a problem, the whole show falls apart! I'd better sort that out now.'

She began to gather up her things and he rose with her.

'I'm working at home today, as you can see. Why not come to the manor and make your call and we can have our first meeting? I can begin to understand what the hell I'm supposed to be doing. We could work through the arrangements if you're not busy.'

Jade walked along the riverbank, thinking furiously. A good full day explaining might be reduce the number of late evening meetings.

'All right,' she said slowly, then her face brightened. She'd kill two birds with one stone. If she *had* to be at the manor, then she might as well use its facilities. 'We'll do it your way. But since I'm doing you a favour, I want one in exchange. I'd like to use the library whenever I want.'

'What for?'

'I'm writing and illustrating a book on the local history,' she said, expecting his scorn.

'Are you?' he said slowly, sounding interested. 'How far have you got? Past the planning stage?'

'I'm up to the medieval period. I've written about forty thousand words,' she said with conscious pride. 'Can I use the library?'

'Not whenever you fancy. Check with me first. It could be in use already.'

'The woman who's staying with you?' she asked lightly, her throat dry and her heart pumping like mad.

'Yes,' he said curtly. 'She has priority. But apart from that, I see no reason why you can't work in there.'

'Well, I was thinking of selecting what books I wanted and working in the studio,' she said hesitantly.

'No. It's in use and you're not to go in there under any circumstances.' He sounded very emphatic.

Jade felt vaguely resentful about that, and rather disappointed. She loved the studio and it would have been ideal, but the library would have to do.

The inside of Saxonbury had been transformed. Whereas she and Sebastian had never even arrested the gradual decline that had begun under the previous owner, Dane had completely restored it to its former glories.

Jade paused in breathless admiration in the hallway, feeling as if she had stepped back into the eighteenth century.

'Oh, Dane!' she cried, clasping her hands in pleasure and turning ther delighted face to his. 'It's lovely! It's—it's so *right*!'

His dark face lit up. 'Thank you. I was worried you might not like it.'

'Like it? You've given Saxonbury back its dignity. I'm so glad. Where did you get all that lovely furniture—and those fabulous oil paintings?'

'My family,' he said dismissively. Then his mouth quirked. 'I come from a long line of Kings.'

Jade's laughter pealed out. 'I bet you've been waiting for an opportunity to say that,' she grinned.

'Rehearsed it for weeks,' he chuckled. 'Come to my study.'

He led the way to the room which had been Sebastian's den. She was a little nervous, wondering what her reaction would be to go in there, but it was so different that it didn't touch her emotional wounds at all.

'Like this, too?' he asked hopefully.

'Very much. It's just right.' It was like him, too: two-sided. Parts of it were well ordered and neat, parts in chaos. His very duality was something she had to come to terms with if they were to work together on the Garland Day. After all, she was complex as well. To some people she might seem free, independent and unrestrained by social rules. Yet she was very strict with herself and others as far as morals were concerned—that always surprised everyone.

Perhaps Sebastian had been right when he'd said she promised more than she delivered. It could be that her naturally loving and expressive temperament clashed with her dislike of coarse behaviour.

'Here's the number of the hirers.'

'Oh, thank you.' She took the phone from him and began to dial, discovering to her dismay that the cheap marquee had been badly damaged by a fire and would not be available on the day they'd booked. When she told Dane, he didn't seem too worried.

'Book another one.'

'That's no good. It's too late, they'll all be spoken for.'

'I'll get one,' he offered.

'Hmm. But could we afford it?' she asked. 'We need it two days before the show: the day itself and the next. That costs.'

'Free?'

'Don't be . . .' She saw he was serious. 'How . . .'

'Never mind. I can do it. A man in my line of business has all kinds of contacts. Shall I go ahead?'

Stunned by his conjuring trick, Jade nodded, leaning back in the comfortable leather chair and watching the way he operated as he organised exactly what he wanted. He was a man who always got his own way. Smoothly, firmly, charmingly. She sighed.

'What's next?' he asked crisply.

Jade explained the procedure and he wrote everything down for next time when he was in charge. She had already booked the Silver Band and the judges, organised the stallholders and the operators of the sideshows. Dane proved to be very imaginative when it came to ideas for prizes, and promised to ask leading firms to present goods as a public relations exercise. Jade had no doubt that he'd persuade them!

'You have to remind the farmer to keep his cows out of Jubilee Meadow and to get it cut and cleared,' she said. 'And check the posters are up three weeks before—they've already been printed.'

'Pity,' he said, looking at the list of activities.

'Why?' she asked, bridling a little. She'd been very organised and efficient!

'I have a couple of ideas you might like to try out.'

'Like what?' Tradition was tradition, and if he tried to alter the format and make it a slick event then that would be awful.

'You've got some nutty events, like Welly Wanging, which I assume is throwing a wellington boot,' he said thoughtfully. 'But we could do more—they're always popular with people who take part, as well as onlookers. I see from the plan that there's a kind of arena in the middle of the outside stalls, where the pony rides take place. How about doing something like a musical mower ride?'

Jade looked puzzled and Dane leaned forwards to explain, his face animated. 'If we could get hold of enough motor mowers, they could do a kind of formation dance to waltzes——'

'And get in a hopeless muddle when the band play a rumba,' laughed Jade, her eyes sparkling. 'It's a great idea—and you can organise it,' she added. 'Good practice. Anything else?'

It seemed that she had opened the flood-gates with that query. Many of Dane's suggestions were so bizarre or radical that they'd need to be tried out gradually over the next few shows, but some were inspirational. They had passed the whole morning, tossing back ideas, sparking off each other, laughing a great deal and thoroughly enjoying being together, before they realised it was way past lunch time.

'Look at the time!' gasped Jade. 'I'm stopping you from working—and I have to eat, even if you don't!'

'I've dealt with a couple of urgent problems,' he said, referring to three phone calls he had handled with swift efficiency. 'Let's finish sorting out what items we expect the children to make for the craft prizes over lunch. There's more than enough for us both to eat in the kitchen.'

'Oh, no,' she demurred. 'I don't want to encroach on your . . .'

'Please. I hate eating alone.'

Alone? She wondered what he'd done with his woman. She oughtn't to have lunch with him, but there were things still to discuss, weren't there? 'Well, in that case . . .'

'Good. Let's raid the larder.'

She followed him with a smile at his enthusiasm and watched doubtfully when he piled an enormous quantity of food on a tray. Mrs Love certainly believed in keeping Dane well fed!

'Is there always such a massive selection of home cooking?' asked Jade, as he tried to find room for a herb quiche.

'I get ravenous during the day. It's something to do with talking a lot on the phone. As long as I have something to nibble, I'm happy,' he said, his eyes slanting at her.

'Don't spoil things,' she warned.

'I just wondered how hell was these days,' he murmured, carrying the tray past her and out to the terrace.

She followed, a little irritated. He had a mistress at his beck and call; was he becoming restless and in need of a challenge? She was disappointed in him, too. All morning she had liked him, admired him even. His terrible reputation had been completely forgotten. Now he'd made her remember that he had feet of clay.

'No change,' she answered, meeting his eyes and wishing they didn't melt when they looked at her.

'You are a fool,' he said quietly, transferring dishes to a low table.

She flushed. 'Because I don't clutch my hands in rapture when you deign to show a sexual interest in me?' she asked hotly.

'Because we get on so well together, have the same sense of humour, enjoy the off-beat world, and for all the other reasons I've mentioned before and am damned if I'll list again.'

'How about a model of a windmill?' she suggested, pushing the craft list towards him and sitting down primly.

He was about to reply when a woman's voice began to call his name from somewhere inside the house.

'Excuse me,' he said, a worried expression on his face. 'Please start. And don't go. We ought to finalise that list today.'

She glared and tucked into the tasty feast, eating far too much because he was gone ages. Gradually a cold anger came over her as she began to wonder just what he was up to. Jealously gnawed at the pit of her stomach. He must have decided he wasn't going to get anywhere with her and was making the most of his guest's availability.

The idea made her feel sick. If it wasn't for the show, she'd leave. When he did appear, she searched his face for signs of lipstick, and then remembered the woman didn't wear make-up. She was probably still in her night things, Jade thought scornfully, and trembled at the pain that ripped through her body.

'Managed to drag yourself away?' she asked coldly.

His blue eyes flared in irritation. 'I think it's time you knew about my guest.'

'Not another sister?' she scorned, hiding her misery.

'Come into the studio,' he said coldly.

'No thank you. I don't want to meet her,' she said with dignity, recoiling at such an idea with horror. What was he up to? Had he no tact? Or was he trying to teach her a lesson—show her that he could get along without her very well?

'You won't. She's not there. She's packing. But you'll be able to see what she's been doing all this time.'

'I hope you didn't use my presence to force her out,' snapped Jade. 'If you pretended that we . . .'

'Will you come, or do I have to drag you?' he yelled suddenly, making her jump.

She rose with ruffled pride and tilted her small chin, giving him a hostile glare.

'You touch me and I'll throw the quiche at you', she threatened.

'That'll be good practise for the coconut shy,' he murmured, motioning her ahead.

Jade's mouth twisted and she made her brows knit together in a false frown. The studio looked as if a bomb had hit a typing pool. A desk had been erected in the middle of the room and on it, from it, under it, and everywhere she could see, were sheets of typewritten paper.

'She's been trying to write you a farewell note all this time?' she hazarded.

'Getting warm,' he replied, leaning against the door-jamb and stuffing his hands in his pockets. 'Go and read a page or two.'

'There are hundreds to choose from,' she observed, picking one and beginning to skim-read. She stopped and went back to the top of the page, finished it, noted the number at the bottom and began to search for the next.

'Don't do that,' he advised. 'You'll be here for days. Well?'

'It's fascinating,' she marvelled. 'Who's Prince Stanislav and why . . .'

'Don't,' he groaned. 'I've lived and breathed the damn thing for the last two years. Now it's finished and all I want to do is get a girl in to get the pages together and send it off.'

'You're not explaining very well,' said Jade, pushing aside scattered paper and clearing a space on a comfortable settee. Too late, she realised that she'd made enough—just enough—space for Dane and he was settling down beside her, his thigh against hers.

'She's an author,' he said, stretching out his long legs in front of him. 'I can't tell you her name because she shuns publicity and you'd know who she was immediately. You see, she had a best-seller out a few years ago and since then had been unable to write. It nearly drove her mad. Then she presented me with a synopsis and a few chapters two years ago, and I negotiated an advance for her on the strength of that. It was obviously going to be another blockbuster, and ever since then the publishers have been nagging as she missed deadline after deadline. She just couldn't write the last few chapters. Eventually I suggested she tried a change of scenery and came to the depths of the country to work. For some reason, the environment released her of tensions and the words poured out.'

'I see,' muttered Jade, looking around the chaotic room. What a way to work!

'I sheltered her, shielded her, comforted her and occasionally nagged her,' he said.

A flush burnt her cheeks. 'Hugged her?' she queried, remembering the episode when she had been collecting her bees.

'Of course,' he said softly. 'We all need hugging when we're feeling low.'

Jade winced. There had been too many occasions lately when she would have loved a hug from Dane.

'I never slept with her, Jade.'

'It's none of my business what you do with your authors,' she said haughtily.

'It is,' he said, his eyes holding hers. 'You'd hardly let me kiss you if you thought another woman under this roof was also being seduced by me.'

'Also?' she said huskily. 'There's no also about it!'

'I'm sorry. I'm not saying this very well——'

'Yes, you are. You're telling me that you can spend weeks in the same house as an attractive woman and not make love to her,' she said in tones which showed she didn't believe a word he was saying.

'It's true!' he roared, grabbing her arms angrily and giving her a little shake. 'Somehow I've got to get it into your dense skull that I'm not a rake!'

'Well, that's not the way to do it!' she raged, indicating his tightly gripping hands.

'Jade, I am not, repeat *not*, promiscuous——'

'Why on earth should you imagine that your sex-life has the slightest interest for me?' she queried. 'I don't want to know what you get up to in the privacy of your home or wherever else you choose to enjoy all these women who flow in and out of here like lambs to the slaughter,' she continued, getting into her stride and about to launch into a tirade of reproof.

'Jealous?' he asked slyly. 'You've been glued to your window, watching?'

'Certainly not!' she denied. 'I'd have to have my head stuck in the soil not to notice the turnover in women here.'

He laughed, his hand gently caressing her shoulders. 'They're all my authors, Jade. All here on business.'

'All women,' she sneered.

'Most are. They're my speciality.'

'I'll bet!'

'For a woman who doesn't care if I'm celibate or a sex maniac, you're getting very aerated about the subject,' he murmured.

'Damn you, Dane King!' she seethed, trying to rise. His

hands thrust her back.

Her angry expression made him even more amused, and she pushed hard at his chest, expecting him to give way, but he merely ignored her struggles and hauled her roughly against his body.

'Enough,' he muttered, his lips parting hungrily. 'Time for dessert.'

Jade's head snapped back, exposing her vulnerable throat. 'You'll get your just deserts in a minute,' she threatened.

Dane laughed wickedly and his mouth surrounded the soft hollow at the base of her throat, making her moan out loud.

'Better than quiche,' he breathed, catching her chin between his tumb and forefinger. 'Much better.'

'No——' Her protest was ignored. Dane growled low in his throat and lightly traced her cheekbones with his mouth. Desire flared in his eyes and, with a muttered exclamation, his lips claimed hers in a deeply passionate kiss that made her heart soar and her body throb.

When he pulled back to see her reaction, Jade's eyes were feverish. He had awoken her again, aroused such a clamour within her that she was having terrible difficulties in crushing them. He was nuzzling her bare shoulder, slipping the narrow strap of her top down and her limbs were too leaden to prevent him, her voice caught somewhere in her throat and imprisoned by desire.

'Oh, God, Jade!' he muttered into her silken skin. 'I can't believe this is happening at last!'

His warm, gentle lips kissed across her collar-bones and then he pushed her back on the settee, half lying across her, his mouth lightly brushing hers, as he watched every emotion that flickered in Jade's half-closed eyes. His hands were doing things to her body that had her crying out both in protest and need.

Their breath mingled, hot, erratic, heavy. Dane's passion was evident from the way his kisses were becoming more insistent, more frantic and uncontrolled, and she made half-hearted effort to push away his intimately searching hands as they slid under her brief top.

'No, don't stop me,' he groaned. 'Let me touch you, Jade. Like . . . this.'

The effect of his tentative fingers was electrifying, sending rivers of heat through Jade's body and, as she arched her back, she brought her breasts into his hands. A long shudder was drawn from him and impatiently he fumbled with her buttons at the front, kissing Jade madly while he did so. She was so overwhelmed by the sudden erotic flicker of his tongue and in answering his thrusting exploration with an eager response of her own, that he had bared her breasts before she realised.

And then it was too late. His mouth left hers and he slid down slightly, his lips finding her tight, engorged nipple and moistening it delicately. Jade wanted more. Her hands flew to the back of his head and she twined her fingers through his black curls, pressing him harder into her breast, trying to tell him that her need was urgent and fierce.

She felt his teeth gently grazing, then he began to suckle, gently at first and then strongly, transferring his mouth to the other breast. Jade could hardly bear the sweet agony. She wanted to kiss him very hard, and yanked his hair. Knowing exactly her need, he moved up and claimed possession of her mouth roughly, with a savagery that took her breath away till her lips felt swollen and bruised and other parts of her body were writhing for his touch.

Dane pulled away, ripping at the buttons on his shirt, frowning in impatience as they refused to part under his trembling fingers. Jade reached up, and between them they removed it.

'Oh, Dane,' she whispered, slowly spreading her hands on his big, muscular chest and exploring its feel, the hardness, the strength, its satin skin and the neatly curling black hairs. Her fingers took their time while he stayed very still, gazing down on her with tender desire. And then, as her touch slid lower, his self-control began to slip.

'Undo my belt,' he said hoarsely.

She bit her lip and looked at him from under her lashes. 'Dane, I——'

He closed his eyes in pain, then bent to kiss her, a coaxing teasing kiss, that at once ignited her and brought her to the edge of surrender. His lips and hands began to wander, seemingly everywhere, touching, kissing, nibbling, murmuring, stroking, until she was in such a frenzy of desire that she abandoned herself to the pleasure and wanted to touch him too, enjoying the feel of his body under her hands.

A sudden thrill ran through every nerve as Dane's searching fingers slid between her thighs and moved in an insistent, tantalising rhythm.

'No, I can't, not that,' she breathed.

'You've gone this far,' he said softly into her ear.

'I know, but . . . I don't want——'

'You want me,' he growled. 'If I know anything, it's that.'

'Yes, I do,' she wailed. 'But I don't *want* to want you, and I'm not letting you make love to me!'

The moving fingers took on a fiercer rhythm, and pulses in her body vibrated to fever-pitch.

'We've gone too far to stop now, ' he husked. 'You're close to the edge, aren't you?' he crooned seductively. 'You are as hungry as I am, as starved as I am. It's a long, long

time since I made love to a woman, Jade, and I need you
badly. You've encouraged me to this point.' His mouth
brushed hers tenderly and his eyes kindled as her head
started to thrash from side to side at the primitive beat of
her body. 'Jade!'

One hand moved to undo the tie on her wrapover skirt.
Jagged breath caught in Jade's breast at the look on his face,
and she knew she couldn't fight her own body any longer.
She loved him, whatever his morals, whatever his lies; at
this very moment she wanted him to take her and satisfy the
raging pagan need that dominated every cell of her body.

She lifted her hips so he could slip her skirt away and
remove her briefs, gasping at the exultant light in his face
and the heavy pounding of his heart beneath her splayed
hand.

For a moment he was still, devouring her body with his
eyes, and then his wondering hands touched, trailed in a
glorious torment and she refused to delay her satisfaction
any longer. With an abandoned gesture, she parted her legs
in invitation, thrilling to the shudders which ran through
his body as she did so.

Watching her all the while, he unbuckled his belt and she
closed her eyes tightly, unable to bear the wait. Then his
naked body lay on hers, hot, beating with restrained energy
as he enjoyed the experience of being skin to skin with her,
drinking up the sensation.

Jade wriggled a little.

'So, Jade,' he whispered thickly, 'do you want me?'

'Oh, God!' she moaned. 'Don't torture me! Yes! Please,
Dane . . .'

With a guttural grunt of satisfaction, he raised his hips
and Jade's eyes flew open at the unbearably gentle thrust of
heat within her.

And then, for a long time, Jade was powerless in his arms as he plunged deeper and deeper, sending her wild with the way he moved and teased till she was beside herself with violent hunger and was matching him with thrusting hips, trying to make him lose control, writhing, acting like a wanton and revelling in the wickedness of her seductive movements.

Distractedly, he struggled to stay under control, slowly, gloriously losing the battle.

'Jade!' he said in a choking voice.

To her, it was a call from within, a call which reached the deepest part of her, a call from a man who needed her with a greater and more powerful intensity than anything she could ever have imagined. It echoed what she felt in her heart, and that was the moment she gave everything. Everything.

He sensed she had reached the final point, as he had done, and released the reserve of energy in his body, so that the shock made her head spin and the spiralling crescendo swept through her body in wave upon wave. She began to shudder, running her hands down his back which was bathed in a film of sweat. As she touched his thighs, he trembled and then moved again, and Jade could barely breath as the sensations began again, their gasps of pleasure turning to groans as the savagery of his long-starved virility took over and demanded seemingly endless satisfaction.

Finally, after Jade had found herself moving sinuously to extend her own pleasure and revive his, and he had laughed and called her a seductress, they sank back in utter exhaustion, totally sated.

Dane struggled to get more comfortable, covering her face with small kisses, his mouth slow and drowsy. Tremors still rippled in her feet, making them tingle, and she made little sounds in her throat at each one. He propped himself up on one elbow and looked at her. Neither of them spoke, but gazed solemnly into each other's eyes.

'That was no hell,' he said softly. 'That was paradise.'

'Mmmm.' Jade was drifting off to sleep, and could hardly stop her lids from dropping.

Dane smiled tenderly and kissed her forehead, her nose, and then shut her eyes with light kisses.

CHAPTER SEVEN

WHEN she began to stir after a heavy, dreamless sleep, Jade couldn't think where she was for a moment. Dimly her brain registered that she was in her studio and someone was moving behind her head.

It had happened like that before. She'd been in Sebastian's study and woken from lovemaking—or rather he had made love to her—and he had come up to her as she'd struggled awake and hit her repeatedly, calling her all the names under the sun for not wanting him, for fighting him to the bitter end. The nightmare had returned.

Terror confused her brain. 'Not again,' she moaned. 'Not again, Sebas . . .' There was an indrawn breath, harsh and rasping; she sat up, clutching her skirt which had been draped over her. Slowly her head swivelled around, to see Dane, intense anguish on his face.

'You'd better get dressed,' he said shakily. 'If you want to shower, go ahead. You know there's one off the studio.' He made to walk away.

'*Dane!*'

'Don't bother to explain,' he said, his face drawn into harsh lines. 'I thought . . . I think I've been the fool.'

'*No——*'

'Oh, yes,' he growled. 'A fool to think you had forgotten your husband. One of these days, Jade Kendall, you'll get arm-ache, carrying that damn torch for him!'

'Oh, he always comes between us . . .' she moaned in misery.

121

'He does, doesn't he? Even when we . . . oh, hell! I suppose a woman can get as sex-starved as a man. I must confess, I didn't think you were using me. That make us quits, I suppose.'

'Quits?' she whispered, dreading his next words.

'Of course,' he said, looking her up and down. 'We did each other a favour. We were both in need of relief, after all.'

'R-r-relief?' Jade was appalled.

'Look,' he said, chewing his lip, 'this has taken up rather a lot of time. Do you mind if we skip sorting out the children's craft items? Perhaps another evening.'

She was open-mouthed in outrage and quite unable to answer for several seconds.

'I'm sorry!' she spluttered eventually. 'I would have been a little quicker if I'd realised you were so busy!'

'I think we both needed every second we took, don't you?' he said, lifting his head proudly. 'Still, now you've solved your little problem for a while, you can return to your memories, can't you? One thing: don't call on my . . . er . . . services again. I prefer to know where I stand *before* I make love to a woman, not after. Excuse me. I need a thorough shower.'

Jade was horrified at the misunderstanding. He had been deeply hurt and that hurt her, too, despite his cruel words. She almost prevented him from leaving, almost explaining why she'd begun to say Sebastian's name, and then it dawned on her that maybe it was for the best if Dane thought she pined for her late husband.

It meant that he wouldn't flirt with her, touch her, kiss her, seduce . . . Knives twisted in her chest. Dane's lovemaking had been the most incredibly erotic and satisfying experience in the whole of her life. Every part of her body had felt at peace, complete, content. He now had her heart and soul; he possessed her completely. She loved him, but it was a painful kind of love.

For there was that nagging doubt in her mind. A man like Dane King could have his pick of women—and probably did. She couldn't see him being satisfied with her, and she certainly didn't intend being one of his casual flings. Far too many women had gone in and out of his life recently, and she'd been a fool to put herself on the list.

But he was such a seducer!

Jade groaned at the memories and the burning of her body. She swung her legs to the floor and staggered to the small bathroom which had been built on to the studio for her use. Every drop of water that beat on her body seemed to throb to the same pitch as her molten loins. Oh, Dane, she whispered, soaping her body carefully, trying not to handle her sensitised breasts too much—Dane, I wish I didn't feel this way about you!

For Jade knew that if he walked in right at that moment, she would be powerless to deny him, despite the almost total exhaustion of her body. She wanted to drown in him, to give herself again, to share his nights.

Trembling from weakness, she dried herself and dressed, blushing when she saw how far he had tossed her skimpy top in his abandon. And she slowly made her way home across the lawn, taking the short-cut, tumbling awkwardly over the low flint wall into back garden and crawling up the stairs to bed, even though it was only early evening.

She wasn't even able to sleep out her exhaustion. Loud squawks woke her. Lurching from the blackness of sleep to find that it was now late at night, it took many shaky moments before her mind focused and she began to recognise the clucking of her hens.

Fear clutched at her stomach. It was either a poacher or a fox. And if Polly wasn't barking, then it was a poacher and he had drugged her dog! Jade's fertile imagination began to race ahead, till she shook herself impatiently.

There were several things she could do: ringing the police being the first option. But it would take them a long time to come from Lewes. Then she could ring someone else, like Charlie.

The squawking grew more frantic. Naked in the moonlight, she ran to her wardrobe and drew on a flying suit. The fox—or poacher—would be clean away by the time any neighbours arrived. There was nothing for it but to cope alone. She zipped up the jumpsuit and half tumbled down the stairs.

Cursing Dane for the exhaustion of her body, she forced her trembling hands to lift out the heavy stick she kept by the back door and crept down the path. The noise was terrible and she began to think it must be a fox, after all.

At that moment, Polly came bounding over the wall; she'd been rabbiting, or something, thought Jade crossly, grabbing her collar and gripping her muzzle. Together they advanced towards the enclosure. Feathers were flying everywhere and she smelt a musky scent. She let Polly loose, there was a yelp and a small, skinny red shape flashed past, streaking through a gap in the wire-mesh fence around the chicken pen and over the fields, with Polly in hot pursuit.

Jade sat down on the earth in a crumpled, defeated heap. Torn and mangled bodies lay around with a covering of feathers. A few terrified hens clucked hysterically, rushing up and down like maniacs. Wearily she struggled to her feet and shut them in the hen-house, where they calmed down in the darkness.

She ignored the mess and went to bed. Some time she

would have to clear up, but not now. She had to sleep.

In fact she slept late, past ten o'clock. Her body was stiff as she dressed, and it felt tender from Dane's lovemaking. In a daze, refusing to think about anything, she made breakfast, and only then did she try to concentrate on her next actions. One thing at a time. Chickens first.

She'd have to sort out the chaos. Dreading the idea, she walked slowly down the garden. Her weariness lifted at the sight of Dane, waiting for her.

'I didn't like to wake you,' he said expressionlessly. 'But I thought you might need help.'

Dejectedly she stared at the enclosure. Right at that moment she had no stomach for doing anything about it.

'Fox, was it?' he asked, studying her carefully.

She nodded wordlessly.

'I didn't hear anything,' he said.

'You must be a heavy sleeper.'

'Sleep?' He gave a mirthless laugh. 'I spent the night driving. I came here to apologise for the things I said to you. I was very angry and my pride had taken a bashing. So perhaps I can do something to make up for my unkind words. What happened? Did you see it?'

'There must be a hole in the enclosure. Polly set off after the fox but failed to catch it. From the look of her when she returned, she'd tried to squeeze into its earth, but she must have been too big.'

'I'm surprised no one in the village heard.'

'You forget, the church and the school are between me and the next row of cottages. Anyway, it was late. Most people with any sense would be deeply asleep,' she said gloomily, wishing she hadn't woken.

'You sound very tired,' he said quietly.

Her scathing glance flashed briefly at him, and then

dropped. She was too bone-weary even to get angry.

'What can I do to help?' he asked.

'You could finish cleaning up the chicken run, go and buy me some more pullets from a reliable source and settle them in,' she said sardonically. 'Other than that, not a lot.'

'All right.'

'Wait a minute!' she cried. 'I didn't mean . . .'

'I know. But you should be careful, saying things you don't mean, Jade. As it happens, I can do all those things for you. Let me take care of this.'

'But . . .'

'Lean on me. Rely on me. Trust me, Jade,' he said quietly, and began to work.

Uncertain what to do, but utterly relieved that he had taken over, she went indoors, sat down to think and fell asleep. She woke very much refreshed, and was horrified to see that she'd slept the morning away.

When she went down to the coop, she couldn't believe her eyes. Everything she had asked for so mockingly had been done. It was impossible!

'Where—Dane, where did you get . . . they are layers, aren't they, I mean . . .'

'You forget, it's Lewes market day. I rang a friend of my father's and he brought them over. Remember, Father was a farmer. You will keep forgetting that I know your kind of life. I know how to look after animals, Jade and how to buy and sell livestock.'

'I—Dane, I didn't expect . . .'

'No. It doesn't fit in with your preconceptions of me, does it, to find me crawling in the dirt, checking for holes in your fence?' he said bitterly.

'No, it doesn't,' she admitted, noticing how filthy he

had become. There was a streak of dirt across his forehead, and she longed to dampen her hanky and wipe it clean. His eyes softened and she felt her lips part as another longing swept through her.

'Oh, God!' she muttered, turning blindly away.

His arms were around her, though, holding her as if he'd never let her go. She leaned her head back into his shoulder and he stroked her hair.

'I wish I didn't like you,' she whispered.

He chuckled and bent down to kiss her ear affectionately. 'Why shouldn't you? I'm a very likeable man.'

'That's what I'm afraid,' of she muttered.

He turned her around in his arms and gazed at her very seriously. 'You're afraid? But, Jade, why aren't you glad? Isn't it enjoyable to discover you like someone—especially if that person wants to build a solid relationship with you.'

Jade wanted to believe in him; she longed to think that he was going to put aside his old life and settle down with her. But inside she knew that was all 'pie in the sky'. He tipped up her chin to see her expression better, and her body quivered. Involuntarily, her lips parted at the stab of desire and love within her, and she knew to her dismay that this had been reflected in her eyes.

'You still think of the past?' he murmured.

Jade closed her eyes tightly, refusing to let herself respond as his hand cupped her face and his fingers lightly feathered her cheekbones.

'Damn you, Jade,' he growled softly.

Her breasts began to rise with her erratic breathing. He could destroy all her resolutions just by standing near, and all she wanted was to have him for always, to be there whenever she needed him, to laugh and share amusing incidents with him, to comfort her when she was feeling low, to be involved in village life together, to love.

'Oh, Dane,' she said brokenly. 'I need you, but you must realise that it's no use . . .'

'Damn him to hell!' he seethed. 'I won't let him take you away from me! I want you; I know you're using me, but I want you!'

His hands were roaming with none of their first hesitation, boldly claiming her body as his right, and she didn't stop him. He looked furiously angry and out of control, and Jade surrendered, telling herself that she couldn't prevent him from doing whatever he wanted, knowing that she was crazy but incapable of denying herself the pleasure of his touch. Fiercely his mouth bruised her lips as she tried to sweep Sebastian from her mind. Then, without a word, he drew her indoors.

'Where's your bathroom?' he asked hoarsely, his eyes avid for her.

'I—there!' she quavered.

He scooped his arm around her waist and half lifted her in there with him, locking the door. Jade looked at him nervously. He was already shedding his clothes. Her hand reached out to the bolt to undo it and she was whirled into his arms, kissed till she could hardly stand and then slowly, very tantalisingly, undressed. All the time her heart pounded against her ribs in excitement and her head tried to make her reject him. But he was too determined, too quick, and so utterly desirable that she found herself stepping under the shower with him and watching in trembling delight as the water ran in fascinating paths over his powerful body.

He handed her the soap with a meaningful look. Jade gulped and he kissed her under the full jet so that she felt she was swimming and floating in a dream. Her dazed mind followed the way her hands cupped and curved over his muscles, as they stood a few tantalising inches apart. When she stroked his hips, he began to breathe heavily, his eyes begging her to touch him.

She hesitated and then reached out, but he only allowed her to trail her finger delicately for a few brief seconds before he snapped off the shower and lifted her hastily on to the thick white carpet and covered her with his body. His teeth bit into her lower lip gently, but there was nothing gentle about the way he looked at her. Jade despaired—both at her own weakness and that he was treating her like all his women, as a convenient vessel for his pleasure.

Angrily she began to fight him, and they rolled on the carpet in a tangle of golden-tanned limbs. Dane easily pinned her to the ground, and glared at her with glittering eyes. His head bent and Jade gasped in shock as she felt the moist warmth of his mouth and the indescribable delicacy of his tongue flickering intimately.

'Oh, no! N-n-no!' she cried helplessly.

He reared above her, darkly angry. 'If it's the last thing I make you do,' he seethed, 'you'll cry out for me. Me, Jade!'

Under his taunting lips, she writhed and moaned, till she no longer fought against him but was trying to lift her hips and make him take her. She was at the point of no return, grazing his shoulder with her teeth, clinging to his broad back and urging him on with every inch of her body.

Then he moved away and his impassioned assault stopped. Hazily she opened her eyes and her pulse beat more rapidly to see his magnificent body.

She gave a little whimper and ran her hands down her body temptingly, delighted at the way he reacted: straddling her immediately and thrusting deeply. Jade sank into him, filling herself as if yesterday had never been, fighting, loving, demanding, and finally calling his name as he had predicted, over and over again till she was fulfilled and snuggling down in the crook of his arm.

A little later he carried her into her bedroom and made love to her again, tenderly, and then a third time with a great leisure and much mutual exploration, introducing her to new delights on each occasion. Jade could no longer stay awake, but fell asleep still linked with him.

A pattern emerged in their relationship. They met at the manor and worked soberly, with Jade intending to reject him outright if he lifted a finger to her. Gradually, during the morning, she would be beguiled by his common sense and efficiency and the easy way they communicated. Then the tension between them would rise until her body was humming from it and she was desperately trying to make herself leave, knowing that she wouldn't.

He would make love to her, fiercely, passionately, with a kind of desperate fury that terrified her when he had finished and lay beside her, staring blankly at the ceiling. Once he forgot to take the phone off the hook because he had reacted so quickly to a look she had flashed him from under her lashes, and she'd had to endure his velvet voice soothing some hysterical female while he crushed her with his body and refused to let her up.

Jade hated herself sometimes, but when he gave her a certain look, or his fingers brushed her breast, she melted. And it was the same for him. They set each other alight as a match to a candle, and it seemed that the flame between them was not to be extinguished.

If that was all, maybe she could have borne it more easily, but they ignited each other in more than sex. Jade found herself inventing more things for them to discuss, and she was aware that Dane often extended discussions—partly to torment her and partly for the pleasure of her company.

Their relationship would have been perfect if it hadn't been for his womanising. It didn't stop. Several times he put off meetings, saying he had to go to London, and came back too exhausted to make love to her the next day.

Jade was in a paroxysm of jealousy then. And twice he had suggested she didn't call round because one of his authors was staying the night. When she looked at him balefully, he stared straight back.

'I am what I am,' he had said quietly. 'Accept that and don't try to tie me down.'

The next time they met it seemed he could hardly wait for her to walk through the door before he was pushing her against it, his mouth devouring hers hungrily. He took her then and there, without undressing, without preliminaries, and, although Jade enjoyed every wild, uncontrolled second, she was left with a fear that this kind of intensity couldn't last.

By the time the arrangements for the Garland Day were almost completed, he had made love to her in most rooms in the house—except his bedroom.

They had finished marking the name-badges for the stewards who would man the car park, when Dane leaned back in his chair and Jade's heartbeat began to race in anticipation.

'I want you to sleep with me tonight,' he said quietly.

'Yes.' How could she refuse him?

'No. I mean properly. In my bed, in my bedroom.'

Her head snapped up in fright. 'No! I won't!' She got up to go, to escape the idea.

'Jade,' he said in a menacing tone, 'if you leave now, then consider our relationship at an end. I'd hoped . . .' He passed a weary hand over his jaw. 'Hell, I don't know what I hoped. But I did think you'd get over . . .' His eyes flashed angrily as she flinched.

'I just can't,' she said in a whisper, miserable to see him so hurt and so furious. His pride must be wounded, she thought. But she dared not let him know she was completely his—he'd treat her like dirt. It was bad enough now, when he was still trying to win her over. What would it be like if he was sure of her?

'If you won't live with me properly, Jade, then I think we'd better stop torturing ourselves. I don't want to hurt you any more. I was a fool to think I could make you forget him. Just do me a favour and keep well away, will you?'

She looked in anguish at his tormented face. It was better this way. He thought she had missed the pleasure of sex and had given herself to him on those terms only. Perhaps, she thought bitterly, he might reflect on how it felt to be used, next time he turned for a few hours' delight from some unsuspecting woman.

'Goodbye, Dane,' she croaked.

His eyes glittered at her for a moment, then as she left the room she heard the table overturn violently. She faltered, but then continued to walk away, hardly able to breathe from the choking emotions.

Like remote strangers, they supervised the setting up of the marquee and the installation of the tables and chairs from the village hall. On the Saturday morning, the exhibits were arranged and Jade was amazed at how smoothly everything went. Normally there was chaos, with people losing their tempers in the summer heat and under the stress of competing. This year, Dane changed all that. He seemed to be everywhere, always speaking softly and reasonably, taking every problem and deflecting it, dealing with it, always reliable and steady.

'Dane.' She had a problem now, and had automatically turned to him. 'One of the judges has made some rather acerbic comments to one of the dahlia competitors. He's threatening to take his display away. Do you think . . .'

'Sure,' he said briskly. 'George!' he smiled a greeting at the competitor, who was bearing down on them, the judge hurrying behind in an evidently bristling manner, intending to put his side of the story.

'This . . . this idiot here, who's probably never even staked a dahlia, let alone——'

'Mr King, if I'm not to be allowed to judge without——'

'Now, look,' said George, belligerently, 'I've been growing dahlias, man and boy——'

'Let's go and have a beer in the beer tent,' said Dane, his strong arms taking hold of the two men in a friendly but firm way. 'You can tell me your side of this, George, and . . .'
They disappeared into the tent. Jade heard raised voices for a moment and a quieter, soothing one, and then a general murmur. After a while, all three men came out laughing.

'How did you do that?' she asked in amazement as George and the judge strode away to the marquee. 'That judge has always been difficult.'

Dane smiled. 'Unashamed bribery,' he said. 'And a few white lies. I looked all puzzled to find the judge doing the dahlias, when I'd intended he should act as supervisory judge this year. Obviously my letter hadn't reached him.'

'What letter? We didn't . . . you fraud!' she giggled.

'I know,' he admitted. 'You had warned me about him. I couldn't tell him we didn't want him any more, he looks forward to this so much in his retirement. He reads up all his old text books and so on for weeks beforehand.'

'That was nice of you,' said Jade impulsively. 'So George was mollified?'

'Well, I persuaded the judge to praise his exhibit and they started talking about collarettes, double-show and disbudding and I bowed out.'

As Jade laughed, there was a yell and a crunching sound. Dane was half-way across the arena by the time she had registered that one of the ponies had taken fright at one of the rehearsing motor mowers and backed into a crucial support for the marquee. She ran over to find Dane taking the strain of the ominously cracking pole and calmly organising men to haul a long section of scaffolding into place as a temporary measure.

'Well done. A bit to the left. Charlie, put your shoulder against the strut. Good. Gently, now. OK.'

'It's holding,' said Charlie. 'You can let go now, Dane.'

'We'll get it splinted first,' he said. 'Find a steel pole, one off the end section of the judge's stand. We can rearrange that after.' He saw Jade nearby, watching him with serious eyes. 'And I thought life in the country was peaceful,' he said ruefully. 'This is one excitement after another!'

She didn't answer. It was too heartwrenching, seeing him so calm, so resourceful, so much in command of everyone, averting crises as if he'd been born to do so. Her love for him swamped her, and she walked out without acknowledging his friendly overture.

All those involved in the morning preparation had a snack lunch provided by caterers at Dane's expense. As Jade sat in the arena, eating the picnic with everyone else involved, at some distance from him, she glumly watched him charming everyone in sight.

Charm. That terrible, devastating smoothness, the easy smile he threw in all directions. He was a compulsive, suave seducer of mankind, she thought sourly.

When the show opened at two o'clock, Jade had no time to think about Dane. She was busy helping out on the produce stall. It had been decided that he was better left free, to roam around and ensure everything was running smoothly and to be on hand for any decisions that needed taking, but Jade hadn't expected him to take his duties so lightly that he found time to wrap his arm around two women and show them the stalls. One of them was the infamous Dodo, the blonde in the diaphanous silk. This time she was in a pale blue shantung suit with enormous shoulders.

Jade's face was tight with tension when he strolled up.

'Oh, look, Dane!' cried Dodo. 'Home-made honey! I must have some!'

'It was made in the garden, actually,' said Jade laconically. 'By bees,' she added, in case the blonde didn't know.

Dane was trying to keep a straight face.

'How about some home-made eggs, too?' asked Jade innocently. 'Hens made them.'

The blonde flushed. 'You know what I meant,' she said sulkily.

'Dane!' Charlie's bellow filled the air, making them jump. He lumbered up and Jade saw the awed look on the two women's faces at his flexing muscles in the tight T-shirt. 'Need your help. Loudspeaker's on the blink and I can't find the electrician. I could shout,' he offered.

'No need,' grinned Dane. 'I can handle it.'

'Oh,' called Charlie. 'The vicar is hurt because no one

has thanked him for setting up the clock golf. And we're running out of change. We've attracted a bigger crowd, and it seems everyone pays with five-pound notes or pound coins.'

'Come with me,' Dane said in a confident voice. 'Sorry, girls, duty calls. Enjoy yourselves.'

Jade discovered she was standing like the two women, ogling Dane as he left, and could have kicked herself. Then Soniver made an appearance and greeted the two women as if they were long-lost friends.

'We were just buying some honey,' said Dodo, searching in her purse.

'If it's anything like the stuff Dane kept sending me,' said Soniver, peering at the labels, 'it's heavenly. Oh, Jade! I didn't notice you there!'

'Hello, Soniver,' she smiled.

'This is Dodo,' said Soniver, 'and this is Harriet. Meet Jade Kendall, Dane's next-door neighbour.'

'Lucky you,' sighed Dodo.

'Oh, you don't seem to be doing too badly,' murmured Jade.

Soniver laughed. 'Dodo and Harriet are part of Dane's stable,' she said, as if that explained everything.

'You make it sound as if he's running a stud,' laughed Harriet.

'Isn't he?' queried Jade sweetly.

'Don't be ridiculous. I told you they're two of his writers,' said Soniver.

'I'm sorry,' said Jade politely. 'I don't see the significance of that.'

'It's his house rule,' pouted Dodo. 'He never mixes business with pleasure. It's almost worth getting another agent under those circumstances. Come on, Harriet, let's see if we can find him.'

'Are you saying,' said Jade slowly to Soniver, 'that he never—*never*—er . . .'

'Makes love to his writers?' murmured Soniver. 'No, of course not. That would be madness.'

'Why?' she breathed.

She shrugged. 'It's too delicate a relationship. He spends half his time chivvying them along in a very subtle and gentle way, and the other half offering them a shoulder to cry on, or giving them advice, or helping to sort out their lives when they get divorced or the children leave home and . . .'

'Wait a minute,' said Jade. 'He's a literary agent, not a social worker!'

'Same thing,' grinned Soniver. 'Dane is at the top of his profession and has become all things to all men. And women. He's reliable, Jade, you must know that by know. He's the kind of man women lean on. He is interested in them and their problems, and has a flair for making their lives run smoothly so they can get on with the important business of writing. But you must *know* that.'

'Why must I?' she asked, her heart thudding.

'Because he's head over heels in love with you and I can't imagine you spend *all* your time making love and never talking,' said Soniver.

Jade's eyes widened to their full extent. 'I—I——'

'Sorry,' she grinned. 'Dane says I get a bit basic at times. I dislike beating around the bush. I'm going to have a go at the coconut shy. Haven't done that kind of thing for years. See you.'

Jade was left with her astonishment, her mind reeling. Soniver was deluded! Whatever had given the impression that Dane had anything more than a sexual interest in her?

And, come to that, she thought angrily, how dared he tell Soniver about her?

She chewed over the information about his 'stable' of women. Curiosity welled up within her. Suddenly she decided to do a little market research. She called over one of the stewards and asked if they'd man the stall for her. In the background she could hear the music striking up 'The Blue Danube' for the Motor Mowing Musical Ride. She marched to the arena where everyone was gathering and searched out her quarry.

'Hello again,' she said pleasantly to Dodo.

'Aren't they good?' she gurgled.

'I was just wondering, have I read any of your books, do you think?' asked Jade.

Dodo beamed. 'Dorothy Vincenzi. I'm a scriptwriter for television. I write *Lovers*.'

Jade nodded as a roar of laughter came from the crowd. They were lapping up Dane's mad idea, it seemed.

'So you write that soap opera. It's terribly successful,' she said. 'You don't get inspiration from Dane, then,' she smiled, fishing.

'Only for the way the hero looks,' sighed Dodo wistfully. 'Dane is utterly charming, but utterly unattainable. I've tried. We've all tried. No one gets anywhere.'

'Oh.'

'Satisfied?' grated Dane's voice in her ear.

She started. 'I wouldn't be surprised if you'd primed her to say that,' she snapped, moving away.

He followed angrily. 'Won't you ever see the truth?' he growled.

Jade stopped dead. 'I want to know why you filled Soniver's head with lies,' she said coldly.

'Lies? About what?'

'Us. You told her we've been . . . we'd . . .'

'Become lovers?' His face was as black as thunder.

'Yes,' she whispered. 'And you tried to make it acceptable by telling her that——'

She bit her lip, unable to say the words. They meant too much to her to be spoken like this.

'Dammit, Jade, I can't keep on interpreting what you intend to say!' he muttered. 'What am I supposed to have said?'

'She is under the misguided impression that you . . . love me,' she said in a barely audible voice.

Dane's faced grew cold, his eyes like chips of glass.

'Soniver can come to what conclusion she pleases,' he said hoarsely. 'I told her nothing. Absolutely nothing. I wouldn't dream of discussing my affairs with her.'

'You swine! How dare you call me one of your affairs!'

'Aren't you?' he scorned.

'*Ohhh!* Why would Soniver say such a thing?' wailed Jade.

'I've no idea,' he snapped. 'Maybe she thinks we're suited to one another.'

'You'd better put her straight,' croaked Jade.

'*No!* You damn well do it!' he yelled, making people turn in surprise.

'Please, keep your voice down,' she begged.

'I'll do better than that. I won't bother to talk to you at all. Excuse me, I have things to do.'

Blushing with embarrassment that their quarrel had been noticed by so many people, she returned to her stall. All afternoon she smiled mechanically, trying to work out the things she had learnt that day. All those woman could have been just visiting, though it seemed far-fetched.

Yet everyone who had denied his involvement with them—including Dane—had sounded perfectly sincere. She didn't want to think he was telling the truth, but deep down she knew he was. That confused her. She found herself incapable of rational thought: round and round in her head went the knowledge that he might not be a philanderer, after all. And if that was so, where did that leave her?

CHAPTER EIGHT

IT WAS nine o'clock that evening and nearly all the clearing up had been completed. Because his mother and father were helping, Billy Love had stayed and latched on to Jade, doing all kinds of little jobs for her. Both she and Dane had worked as if they had the devil in them—in fact, Charlie had to stop her from carrying the trestle-tables to the truck.

'I can do it,' she said fiercely, needing that strenous physical effort to dissipate some of her emotional and physical feelings.

'You shouldn't—'

'Leave me alone!' she yelled at the unfortunate Charlie.

'Put it down,' ordered Dane in a voice that brooked no defiance. 'Do you want the whole village wondering why our quarrel should have upset you so much?'

'Upset?' she seethed. 'I'm furious!'

Charlie stepped forwards and confronted Dane. 'You'd better keep out of Jade's life,' he warned.

'I most certainly will,' grated Dane. 'But unfortunately this village is small and contact is forced on us. I don't welcome it, I can tell you!'

Jade quivered with pain. Why did handsome bastards think they could use you and kick you aside?

'I was in Saxonbury first,' she cried. 'Why don't you go back to the steets of London where you belong? The women there understand your kind of behaviour.'

'Don't make sweeping generalisations,' he growled. 'I have no intention of leaving. Now, stand away from that table and find something else to do.'

'If you're going to be working here, then I will,' she said.
'I have no wish to be near you!'

She was lying. She wanted to fling herself into his arms
and draw his angry mouth to hers. She wanted those hard,
merciless eyes to look at her with tender longing again, and
the harsh lines of his face to become drowsy with love. But
he looked formidable and withdrawn, and she was too
uncertain of herself. He might take her, mockingly, and
then discard her again. And her self-confidence and respect
couldn't cope with that.

Behind her, Dane and Charlie were arguing as they
moved the table. It sounded ugly. For once in his dealings
with others Dane wasn't staying cool and using reason. Jade
realised with a sinking feeling that she was the only person
she'd every heard him lose his temper with. That must
mean something, she thought gloomily. They struck sparks
from one another because they were incompatible.

Then, as she crossed the arena and smiled vaguely at the
farmer's wife who ran the pony rides, she saw the woman
gasp in astonishment and start to run in Dane's direction.

'He's fallen, or something,' she called to Jade.

Whirling around, Jade could only see Charlie, crouching
on the ground, and then she too began to run, easily
outstripping the farmer's wife. Charlie, was bending over
Dane and the big man's eyes looked guiltily at Jade when
she arrived out of breath.

'I hit him,' he said simply.

Her huge eyes flew down to the recumbent figure. Dane
lay stretched out, his face pure and beautiful to her, looking
as if he was peacefully asleep.

'Oh, my dear, what happened?'

Thinking rapidly, Jade jumped up as the farmer's wife

arrived, panting heavily. This was a difficult situation. She couldn't get into explanations now. More helpers turned up.

'It's all right,' she smiled. 'He fell. I think he banged his head on something. Charlie and I will see to him. You carry on. It's nothing, really.'

She hadn't really lied, just turned the truth around for everyone's good. And his head was turning from side to side, indicating that he was just coming around.

'Charlie and I can get him to hospital if we think he needs it,' she said, knowing the St John's Ambulance Brigade had packed up and left an hour ago. 'Please, carry on, you're needed much more elsewhere. He'll be all right, honestly.'

They moved away, casting backward glances at Jade and the two men. She was searching the arena for something to put under Dane's head, but saw nothing. Her heart was thudding violently with anxiety.

'He will be all right, won't he, Charlie?' she asked, kneeling beside Dane.

'I think so. We'll soon know,' he muttered. 'Jade, I am sorry. We got heated and . . .'

Jade sighed. 'Did anyone see?'

'I don't think so. It happened so fast. You look awfully upset.'

'Of course I'm upset!' she muttered.

'You . . . still have some feelings for him?'

She thought Dane's eyelids flickered and decided not to take any chances.

'Don't be ridiculous, Charlie. I've got more sense. I'd be upset at anyone lying helpless like that,' she said crisply.

Dane moaned and his lashes fluttered again on his cheeks. She leant over him, her long black hair brushing his face.

His lids lifted slowly. To Jade's consternation, his eyes grew warm and sultry. He smiled at her and the knives of impossible love slashed cruelly through her heart.

'Jade?' he muttered, puzzled by the anguish of her face. Then his hand lifted to his jaw and in a flash his expression had changed to a cold stone mask. He struggled on to one elbow and Charlie helped him to sit up.

'I'm sorry, Dane,' he said. 'I shouldn't have done that.'

'You pack one hell of a punch,' growled Dane. 'I'll remember not to lose my temper with you next time.' He shot Charlie a baleful look. 'But it really isn't any of your business.'

'You shouldn't have spoken to Jade like that,' he said truculently.

'I speak to people as they deserve,' said Dane coldly. 'And believe me, if I really said everything I thought about Jade, she'd never recover. Help me up.'

She watched the two men mutely. Dane really hated her. He probably despised her for letting him . . . she felt a flush of heat rise to her face at their abandoned lovemaking and gave an inner groan. It was awful, surrendering yourself so completely, becoming so incredibly intimate with a man and then conducting a cold war with him, knowing that when he looked at you he remembered that intimacy, the caressess, the total wantonness of your union.

Jade's shame was complete. But as Charlie tried to make amends for his uncivilised behaviour by helping Dane to a chair, she found herself worrying about how groggy Dane looked. Her love and concern won over pride.

'I'd better take a look at his jaw,' she said briskly to Charlie. If she could ignore Dane and treat him like a lump of flesh and bone, then she could handle her screaming emotions and hammering pulses.

'I'm all right,' said Dane testily.

'Sit still and be quiet,' she said with a sharpness she didn't feel. 'We don't want you keeling over later, when you're on your own in that big house.' The thought made her tremble.

'I'm all right,' he repeated. 'I moved back enough not to take the full force of his punch. He would have broken my jaw otherwise.'

'You were unconscious,' she said, her voice cracking a little in worry. He wasn't going to look after himself, she could see that.

'Dazed,' he said. 'I could hear everything that was going on all the time, although I must admit it was in a kind of fog and I wasn't sure what was nightmare and what was reality. Not till I was in full possession of my senses,' he said bitterly. 'I just needed a moment to gather myself together.'

She looked doubtfully at Charlie, who shrugged.

'Leave me here,' said Dane irritably. 'When I feel OK I'll come and help with the final clearing up. I have to appear at the get-together afterwards—and all of us had better appear to be the best of friends to allay any gossip. Thanks for the remark, Jade, about me hitting my head. You think quickly on your feet.'

'I don't know . . .' she began uncertainly, crushing the delight at his praise.

'Will you both realise that I am all right and I want to be left alone, and the last thing I want for my recovery is you two around?' he glared.

She bristled immediately. 'That's fine by me. Come on, Charlie. Dane's thick skin probably saved him from any damage.'

Again, Jade put all her energies into helping. By the

time the field was clear—apart from the marquee, which would be dismantled by the hire firm the next morning—she was utterly exhausted. She'd cast surreptitious glances in Dane's direction and seen him sitting sullenly in the chair, his legs outstretched, his hands thrust into his pocket as he stared directly ahead. Then later she'd glanced from under her lashes at the chair across the arena and found that it had gone, and Dane with it.

'Jade! Come on, nothing else to do!' called Mrs Love from the marquee entrance.

Remembering Dane's words about acting friendly, Jade walked reluctantly over. At the end of every Garland Day, the helpers who stayed to clear up were always rewarded by the parish council with home-made cider and fish and chips brought in from a Lewes chip shop. It was always a jolly occasion, but Jade was not in the mood. She was drained and yet she'd have to spend an hour or so being cheerful. Worse, she'd have to be charming to the man she loved and hated in equal measures.

The twenty or so people, mainly men, were clustered around Dane, who was regaling them with a story that made the tent resound with laughter. Putting on a bright smile, Jade collected the last bag of fish and chips from Mrs Love and they both went over to join the crowd.

'Hello, Jade,' called Dane, his mouth smiling, his eyes blank. He immediately shifted his attention to the surrounding men. 'Shall we find some chairs? I'm exhausted. We City men aren't used to all this physical work.'

'You pulled your weight as well as the rest of us,' observed the farmer. 'A bit more than some of us, in fact,' he said meaningfully nodding at his two sons, who were chatting up the vicar's two daughters. There was a general laugh as chairs were arranged in a convivial circle and everyone began to delve into the food hungrily.

Dane had imperceptibly motioned Jade and Charlie to join him and they sat on either side, making bright conversation. Although Dane kept up a running commentary on the afternoon's events, causing much laughter with his dry wit and clever tongue, she was aware that he was very tired—perhaps as tired as she.

It was a tiredness more than purely physical. It was a feeling that everything had ended and there was nothing left to look forward to in the future. For Jade, naturally bubbly and optimistic, that was terribly depressing.

Her eyes constantly strayed to the set of the muscles in Dane's thigh as they flexed and moved beneath the tight black jeans. Because of the way the chairs had been placed, in a friendly intimacy, they were very close. Dane's arms, in the short-sleeved red shirt, occasionally brushed hers as he dipped in the bag of chips or manoeuvred the golden crispy cod into his mouth.

She dreaded every movement of his body. Her senses were alive to him, alerted to every breath and exhalation, straining for the faint musky smell of his body that had delighted her nostrils after they had made love. She could detect it now, and the sweet agony that washed through her and turned her body to molten fire was almost unbearable.

Bravely she struggled to keep a cheerful face, hoping no one would notice the sexual tension that she could feel tying Dane and herself in an unholy alliance. He felt it. She saw how his chest was rising and falling faster than before, how his fingers moved rapidly with a kind of anger. He obviously found it infuriating that her body was putting out signals, but she couldn't help it! And she was trying to pretend they were just on amiable terms.

Eventually the nerve-racking meal was over. Jade had forced herself to eat, knowing how weak she felt, but every mouthful had been an effort to swallow.

By some kind of telepathic agreement, she, Dane and Charlie lingered behind till they were the only ones left.

Charlie looked at the tense, grim couple who seemed unable to meet each other's eyes. He went over to Jade, kissed her on the cheek affectionately, nodded to Dane and walked out.

'How do you feel?' asked Jade in a false bright tone.

'Like hell.'

'What . . . what did you say to Charlie, to make him hit you?' she asked, concealing her nervous reaction to his harsh answer.

'Nothing much. I think we'd both been brewing up for some kind of showdown for a long time. He seems to have taken on a protective role towards you. And he made it quite clear that he knew we'd been . . . lovers.' He paused. 'I didn't think *you* were the kind to kiss and tell.'

Jade's lips had parted in an unconscious invitation at the sensual way his voice had caressed the word 'lovers,' totally oblivious of the rest of his words. She raised pleading eyes to him, sure that the pulsating vibrations surging between them must derive partly from his own desire. For a brief moment, she thought a naked hunger flared in his eyes, and then it died.

'Well? Did you tell Charlie about us?' he demanded.

'Before we—before you seduced me,' she said bravely, squaring her shoulders, 'you upset me about something and Charlie wanted to know why I was angry.' She refused to say she'd cried. 'I said I'd been stupid enough to find you attractive briefly and regretted it. I didn't ever tell him we'd been lovers, he must have guessed from the way we behaved. He watches me closely, you know. Besides, we've never been real lovers. You don't know the meaning of the word.'

'I'm tired. I'm going home,' he breathed, staggering a little as he moved.

'Oh! Dane! Will you be all right?' she gulped. 'Do you want me to . . .'

'*No!*' he roared, wincing at the pain in his jaw. 'I most certainly do *not* want you.'

In a furious rage, he stormed into the night. So, thought Jade bitterly, he didn't even feel anything physical for her. She'd risked his scorn by allowing her feelings to surface, and been slapped down cruelly. That was something that wouldn't happen again.

It was her own humanity to her fellow man, she told herself, that kept her awake for a while that night, wondering if he was all right or whether he had sunk into a concussed daze. The only way she could think of checking without getting her head bitten off was to pretend to do some work in the library.

When she spotted the men in Jubilee Meadow taking down the marquee as she fed the chickens that next morning, she lifted her long skirts and scrambled over the wall, hailing one of them.

'Is Mr King around?' she yelled.

'Not seen him. We rang the bell, but there wasn't any answer. Thought we'd get on without him.'

She threw him a nod and hurtled off to the big house, her brows furrowed in anxiety. She shouldn't have left him. Pride or no pride, she ought to have found some way of keeping an eye on him. Maybe Mrs Love would have stopped overnight, or even Charlie . . .

Breathless, she rang the bell. There was no answer. Jade

hopped about from one foot to the other in panic, leaning on the bell for all she was worth. Since it was Sunday morning, Mrs Love wasn't calling in, though Jade could always get the key from her. She wondered what to do. Impulsively, she raced around the back of the house and tried the kitchen door. It was open! He must have been too tired—or too dazed, she thought, in rising hysteria—to lock it.

Jade dashed inside and checked to see if there was any evidence of breakfast dishes around, in case he'd gone for an early morning stroll. Nothing. Taking a deep breath, she pounded up the stairs, two at a time, and then stood panting in an agony of indecision outside the master bedroom.

'Who the hell is that?' yelled a furious voice.

Jade squeaked in horror and turned to race back downstairs again, realising that not only was Dane conscious, but as mad as hell to have his Sunday morning disturbed!

Before she could reach the top of the stairs, his strong hand caught her arm and was twisting her roughly around.

'What are you up to?' he demanded.

Jade stared, paralysed with fear. He had wrapped a small towel precariously around his hips. Apart from that he was naked. His vital masculinity was overpowering. His fury was unmistakable. When she didn't answer, his lips tightened into a thin, hard line and he pushed her into his bedroom, throwing her on the bed. Jade could hardly breathe in panic.

'I said,' he said menacingly, 'what are you up to?'

'I thought . . . I . . .' She gathered herself together. He had no business treating her like that. She'd only been trying to help. 'When you didn't answer the bell, I thought you might be suffering from the effects of Charlie's fist,' she said defiantly, sitting up and glaring at him. 'I wondered whether you were concussed. It's evident you aren't, so if you don't mind, I'll go.'

'I didn't know you cared.'

She cast him a suspicious look from beneath her lashes. The tone had no expression, and she couldn't tell if he was mocking her or not.

'I don't,' she said, tossing her head. 'I was worried that if I left you and you got worse, Charlie might be in trouble and get sued for assault or something.'

'Charlie and you seem pretty attached to one another,' he muttered, moving near so she couldn't get off the bed without pushing him away.

'At least when he kisses me, he knows it's me. You must have the devil of a job remembering what name to cry out in your passion!' she said recklessly.

Too recklessly, she discovered. Hating to be second fiddle, even if he wasn't particularly interested in a woman, Dane obviously decided to show her that he could still excite her. His eyes blazed and he pushed her back on the bed, yanking away the covers so that she lay on the sheet still warm from his body.

The trembling began within her as his glittering eyes locked with hers and prevented her from calling out or even moving. Slowly his face came nearer and nearer, until it was inches away. Then his mouth ground cruelly into hers, forcing it open, taking total possession of it with a desperation that hurt her even as it ignited her.

She found her arms stealing up around his neck and she wriggled down in the bed, as his hands ran up and down her body in that terrible, tormenting eroticism which captured her senses every time. The towel had slipped away. He lay heavily on her, moving against her clothed body sensually, and she moaned in longing.

He rose above her, his eyes hard, and Jade flung her head to one side to avoid the lust and hate, and then her face registered shock. Her body stilled and seemed to close up.

Dane's cruel fingers bit into her chin as he forced her to look at him.

'What hell are you planning now?' he asked hoarsely.

Her dead eyes met his. He searched her face, his expression thunderous.

'*Sebastian!*' he hissed.

Jade couldn't believe that her late husband could still reach out from the grave and affect her life. But something in her physical make-up had made her freeze when she realised she was in the same bed . . . Her eyes closed.

'I'm sorry,' she said in a dull voice. 'I didn't mean to lead you on. We do have some kind of animal attraction between us, don't we?'

She heard him curse viciously, and then the bed rose as he got up. Rustling sounds told her he was dressing.

'It *was* Sebastian you thought of at that moment, wasn't it?' he said coldly.

'Yes,' she answered.

'I fall for it every time,' he muttered. 'You only have to part your lips and I want to kiss you. I think you're right, Jade. There is an animal lust that knows no sense or decency between us. It's something I've never experienced before and I don't like its capacity to destroy. If you don't want to be raped one day, you'd better stop fluttering your eyelashes at me every time you feel in need of sex. Turn to Charlie instead. I'm sure he'll oblige.'

'Oh! You bastard!' she breathed in outrage, jumping off the bed.

'Wait a minute,' he said with a frown. 'What were you

ringing the front door bell for?'

She tried to marshal her thoughts together. What was her excuse? 'I wanted to consult a book in the library,' she said haughtily.

'How much longer will you need the facilities there?' he frowned, buttoning his shirt. 'I think it would be better for both of us if you put in some concentrated work while I'm in London and got your damn book finished.'

'Yes, I will.' It would give her an incentive to work.

'Keep out of my way today,' he snarled. 'I'm not in a good mood.'

'Neither am I', she snapped. 'Don't forget it was you who threw me on the bed.'

'You were ready for me,' he said huskily. 'Don't forget that.'

CHAPTER NINE

WITH a furious, indrawn breath, Jade marched out. For the next few days she worked in the library, making notes for the final three chapters. Mrs Love came in to clean and cook as usual, leaving a meal ready for Dane when he came in. Jade made sure she was never around when he returned, though a couple of times she'd not noticed the time and he drove past her as she was walking back home.

Then one morning he startled her by walking into the library.

'I've got something you might be interested in,' he said curtly.

Jade raised one eyebrow, as if that was hardly likely.

'One of my authors is working on a novel based on the Cluniac Priory at Lewes. She was showing me some manuscripts she'd unearthed and I had copies made.'

He pushed the photostats on to the desk and Jade picked them up, scanning them in fascination.

'As they refer to the village, I thought you'd be interested,' he said in a remote tone.

'Yes, I am. Thank you.' she said politely.

Inwardly, she was excited. The documents described how a huge rabbit warren was set up in the eleventh century, on Coney Hill in the valley, to supply the monastery with meat. Coney was one of two clay mounds which rose in the alluvial plain above the flood levels and which had always attracted interest.

'Harriet is coming down tomorrow to use the library.

You'll have to share it,' said Dane.

'Harriet? I think I met her,' said Jade, remembering the woman at the flower show.

'You did. She'll have more documents which you might want to use.'

When he had gone, Jade studied the papers carefully, her brain mentally re-ordering her earlier chapters. Perhaps she'd better wait to see what Harriet brought before making any plans.

Instead, she continued ploughing on with the final stages of the book, finding it heavy-going. Dane drove away, and she felt safer in the empty house. Knowing that she had a great deal of new work to do now, she stayed on working late and was just walking through the hall on her way out when Dane let himself in. He looked bone-weary, giving her a brief nod and making his way straight to the kitchen for his meal.

Driven by the need to get on as fast as possible, Jade arrived early the following morning, entering with Mrs Love, and tackling her work straight away. Some time later she heard Dane driving off, presumably to meet the train in Brighton.

Mrs Love brought her a coffee and departed to look after Billy, who'd developed mumps. Dane had told her not to worry about coming in till Billy was better, and that he'd manage without her for a while.

Her eyes weary from reading, Jade took her cup to the window-seat and sat there, dreaming, her mind drifting aimlessly. Under Dane's instructions, the gardeners had made the garden into a paradise. The lawns stretched in a luxuriant green sward to the riotous rose garden, where the old bushes and ramblers had been tamed at last and encouraged to produce richly coloured blooms. Geraniums were banked high on the terrace walls, covering them with a profusion of salmon-pink flowers. Everything looked cared for and loved, from the neatly clipped yew hedges to the herbaceous borders, stacked thickly with delphiniums, lupins, and huge daisies of all shades.

A knock at the door awoke her from her pleasant daze, and she prepared to meet Dane and his guest by arranging her face in a faint smile.

He led forward the woman who had barely made an impression on Jade because she was so taken up with Dodo at the time.

'Harriet, this is Jade Kendall. Harriet Jones. I'm going to leave you two,' he said, glancing at his watch. 'I have a call coming in from Tokyo.'

'Give Soniver my love,' smiled Harriet, after shaking hands with Jade in a friendly way. 'Tell her I think she's right.'

'What's that supposed to mean?' frowned Dane.

'Never mind,' grinned Harriet. 'Do as you're told, young man.'

Jade craned her neck a little to look at Harriet more closely. Fine lines marked her brow and the corners of her eyes. Despite the shine of her bobbed brown hair, and the freshness of her complexion, she must be older than she looked. She had a good figure, and the jeans and T-shirt made her look almost girlish, but now she could see that Harriet must be forty-five.

'Can I get you a coffee?' asked Jade politely.

'No thanks. I'm still reeling from the British Rail brew,' she said in her laughing voice.

Jade liked her at once. A rapport sprang up between them and they began to discuss the Norman period and swapped local stories of the time. Harriet helped her to decipher one or two words she hadn't been able to read in the documents, and pulled out a great sheaf of material for her to use, laughing at Jade's groan.

'I know,' grinned Harriet. 'You think you've mastered all the research and suddenly up pops something new that you *have* to include. Awful, isn't it?' she added sympathetically.

'Ghastly. But exciting! Will it bother you, me being in here while you work?'

'No. I could work in Oxford Street if I had to,' she laughed. 'When my head is stuck in a book I'm blind to everything around me. Dane says I give him less hassle than any of his women!'

Jade winced. 'He might find it easier if he took on more men,' she observed tartly.

'That would be a waste of his talent. I don't know if you've seen him in action, but he's incredibly sensitive and perceptive. He knows just when to coax and when to nag and when to listen. Mostly he listens. Poor love. He's working himself into the ground at the moment. Doesn't he look awful?'

'I don't know what you mean,' said Jade warily.

'Well, I hadn't seen him for ages till I came down for the village show. I had a shock when I first saw him. He's terribly run-down and drawn-looking. I told him he looked dreadful and he was too old to prance around like a young man any longer.'

'What did he say to that?' asked Jade, her eyes wide.

Harriet grinned. 'Normally he would have looked me up and down and remarked that I was hardly in a position to talk about getting old. This time he told me to mind my own business. That is not typical. He's under considerable strain. Mind you, I suppose he would be, with all the problems he has on his plate.'

'Problems?' asked Jade, her heart in her mouth. Surely he hadn't opened his mouth to Harriet?

'He's doing too much. That's not unusual, he's always generous with his time and emotional energy. Look at the way he opens his house to us! The poor man had hardly any privacy. When he lived in his London flat the place was alive with women needing comfort. People say he's lucky with his authors, but he knows how to care for them in a way that many other agents don't—or aren't prepared to. I can't tell you what strength he gave me when my husband died.'

'Oh, Harriet!' Jade wished she didn't feel admiration for Dane. It wasn't helping her to forget him.

'To be honest,' said Harriet in a confidential manner, 'part of the reason I've come down here is to send Soniver a report. You see, he's negotiating for an agency in Japan through her, and she's had some very odd telephone conversations with him. He hasn't been able to make decisions, which is most unlike him. Once he snapped at her and refused to talk, and another time he said he was too exhausted.'

'Oh, dear, I hadn't realised,' said Jade, guilty that her attitude had probably not helped. 'I wonder if I ought to stop working here?'

'I don't think that's a good idea,' said Harriet quickly. 'He's very keen for you to finish your book.'

'So he said.'

Once she'd finished, she would be out of his life completely. The prospect filled Jade with despair.

'Enough of this,' said Harriet briskly. 'Time we got down to work.'

With Harriet pouring over the old volumes, Jade felt obliged to follow suit and managed to make a great many notes. But all the time there was the nagging thought in the back of her mind that every word she wrote was bringing her closer to a final farewell to the manor and Dane.

It was very pleasant working with Harriet. The older woman helped her a good deal and sometimes called Dane in, who gave curt, but sound advice. Under their guidance, Jade felt some shape come into the last few chapters and she found herself quite excited with her own writing.

That was probably why she didn't notice for a couple of days that she was under the weather. Half-way through a morning in the library, she was suddenly aware of an ache in her throat and that she felt woozy.

'My, you look flushed,' said Harriet, alerted by Jade's muttered exclamation.

'My neck feels swollen. Oh, Harriet!' she cried, her eyes anguished. 'I *can't* have mumps!'

'Silly. Why on earth should you?' Harriet felt her throat and frowned. 'Your glands *are* swollen. Have you had contact with anyone contagious?'

'Yes! Billy Love, at the flower show!' she wailed.

'Well, let's take your temperature. Stay there, I'll find out where Dane keeps a thermometer.'

Now she felt very odd. Jade slumped on to the desk, her head on her arms. After a few moments, she felt Dane's strong hands raising her so that Harriet could check he temperature.

'Just over a hundred,' said Harriet. 'Now what?'

'We get her to bed and call the doctor.' said Dane. 'The question is, whose bed?'

'Hardly the time . . .' began Harriet.

'Jade, have you anyone who can come and look after you?' he asked sharply.

Her brain swung slowly into operation. 'No relatives.

Mrs Love's got Billy ill. Everyone else around here works full-time. It's coming up to the busy season,' she mumbled.

'Friends?'

All her friends had lost touch with her when she'd married Sebastian. They'd lived such a different life to the one she'd known. Instead of a world of musicians and singers, all off-beat, creative people, she had entered the world of high finance and double-dealing. Gradually her friends had drifted away, finding Jade's new life not suited to their tastes, and the quiet, subdued Jade uninteresting. And after Sebastian's death—well, all she had wanted was for peace and solitude to wash over her in all its healing balm.

'Busy people,' she croaked, her eyes filling. No way would she admit to Dane King that her friends only existed in the village.

'Damn!' Dane chewed his lip. 'She can't live alone in her cottage. She'll have to stay here,' he said. 'You'll be around a bit longer, won't you, Harriet?'

'Two days, that's all,' she answered. 'After that, you're on your own.'

'Can't you——'

'No,' she said calmly. 'Take the week off. It'll do you good. You still look like death.'

'Thanks,' he growled, looking at Jade's lolling figure helplessly. 'This is not very desirable. I don't have much choice, do I?'

Jade groaned at his reluctance.

'Not a lot,' grinned Harriet. 'Who knows? You might come to enjoy it!'

He flung her a withering look and picked Jade up, carrying her to the guest-room. Harriet undressed her and they both fussed around in the room, trying to think of things she might need there. The doctor arrived, diagnosed mumps, warned them that it might be severe in an adult woman, and banned Dane from the room.

'I've had mumps. Ten years ago,' he declared.

'Hmmm. Any . . . complications?' asked the doctor delicately.

'I'm not sterile, if that's what you mean,' muttered Dane.

'Fine. You can help to look after her. Now, young lady,' said the doctor, 'do as you're told. Plenty of fluids, take these pills, and rest. You're going to be infectious for a week, so stay put. You might find other glands swelling and you could be quite uncomfortable. Any trouble, give me a ring.' He was about to leave when he turned as an afterthought struck him. 'You're not pregnant, are you?'

Jade felt herself redden. 'No!' she said, embarrassed. Dane had taken that responsibility, thank goodness. She was aware of Harriet's interested face and blushed again.

'Good. Cheer up. It's soon over.'

Jade watched gloomily as Dane escorted the doctor from the bedroom. Harriet made her as comfortable as possible and sat with her till she said she wanted to sleep.

It was evening when she woke, feeling terrible. Her glands were aching dreadfully and there was a dull sensation under her arms. From bleary eyes, she gazed at Dane, who was sitting by the bedside and working through a manuscript. She reached shakily for the glass on the bedside table.

'Let me.' Dane plumped up the pillows and put his hands under her arms to lift her up, looking at her anxiously when she protested. 'Does it hurt there?' he asked gently.

She nodded and took the drink of water from him gratefully.

'What about something to eat?' he asked.

'No.'

'Harriet went out and bought some of those liquid diets. Fancy trying one?'

'No.'

'OK,' he said cheerfully. 'Anything you want?'

'Polly!' she cried, suddenly realising. 'She . . .'

His hands pressed her back to the pillows. 'Relax. I've taken care of everything. Harriet is walking her and then she'll feed her. Polly can stay here. She's used to being in the manor, after all. I've checked the hens and I'll feed them in the morning. I told the bees you were ill,' he said with a twinkle in his eye, 'and they seemed to think they could manage without you.'

'The eggs.' Jade could only manage to say the essential words, her throat hurt so much.

'I collected what there was and I'll do the rounds tomorrow,' he said. 'There's nothing for you to worry about.'

But she did. She worried that he looked exhausted and, whenever she woke during the next two days and caught sight of his face before he noticed her, he seemed as drawn and strained as Harriet had claimed.

Knowing that Harriet was due to leave, she didn't like to mention how awful Dane looked and how much he was doing, because it might seem as if she was trying to make Harriet feel guilty about leaving. And when she did go, Dane took the brunt of the work, driving himself relentlessly

Tossing restlessly in the early hours Jade saw that he was leaving the house just after dawn to see to the hens and that he hardly seemed to stop all day, constantly checking that she was all right, running up and down the huge flight of stairs far too often. Jade tried to manage her own needs as much as possible, but she grew gradually worse, and one day she was very feverish, her body on fire.

'A hundred and three,' frowned Dane. 'You'd better take an extra dose of the pills, as the doctor said, and I'll cool you down.'

He went off and reappeared with towels and a large bowl of water. Up to now, Jade had sponged herself down. She realised she hadn't the strength today, but wasn't prepared to let him touch her!

'No, Dane,' she mumbled.

'Don't be stubborn,' he said cheerfully. 'Doctor knows best.'

'No . . .' Her hot, sticky hands swept over her sweating brow. 'Leave me alone.'

'Not yet, you can do your Greta Garbo act later,' he said, still in the same brisk tone. 'Up we come.'

'*We're* not going anywhere,' she glared.

'All nurses talk like that,' he said. 'It makes the patients feel comforted.'

'Makes me furious,' she muttered, flinging an arm above her head. 'Open a window, please, I'm hot.'

'No. I went and had a chat with Mrs Love today,' he said in a conversational tone. 'She gave me all sorts of tips. You're having the bed-bath treatment she recommended. If you object, you can take it up with her later. Now, I haven't done this before, so it might take a while. But you'll feel a lot better afterwards.' He paused, eyeing her doubtfully as she flung her head restlessly from side to side. 'Whatever it might do to me,' he muttered under his breath.

'Go away.' Her head ached and she wanted peace.

'Yes, of course,' he said, ignoring her.

Gently he bathed her fevered brow, pushing her hair up and over the pillow, away from her neck. The cool flannel felt marvellous. Jade shut her eyes, revelling in the slow, soothing strokes. He dried her face, and then she felt fresh air on her breasts and looked down to see that she was naked to the waist. Her huge eyes gazed mutely at Dane, whose jaw was clenched tightly as he concentrated on cooling her down. He lifted her arms gently and Jade gave herself over to his administrations.

She was too weak to protest as he washed her hips, thighs and legs, and allowed him to turn her over without demur. After, she lay refreshed and glowing, an odd, hazy sensation in her head and a tingling throughout her body where he had touched her.

'I'll change the sheets tomorrow morning,' he said curtly. 'I think that's enough for now.'

'Thank you.' He seemed unable to tear himself away. Jade felt her head swimming and fought for sanity. 'How's my animals?' she croaked.

'Fine. I'll give Polly a run now. Will you be all right?' He turned haunted eyes on her, dark-circled and distant.

'Yes.' She wanted to apologise for being such a nuisance, to ask him to find someone to do all this instead, but he had stalked out.

That night, she became worse. Dane spent half the night holding her, bathing her and trying to help her to cope with the pains near her breasts. His voice and his light touch did a great deal to help, and she must have fallen asleep in his arms, because she woke to find herself sharing the bed with him as he sprawled in a heavy sleep across her.

Hazily she stroked his tumbled hair, cradling his head on her breast, daring to kiss his forehead lightly and run her hands down his broad back. He'd flung off his shoes but was still wearing his shirt and thin cotton jeans, and Jade's heart flooded with love at the boyish way he slept, taking the whole bed with his splayed legs, one fist doubled up fiercely, his mouth sulky with sleep.

In the distance, her cockerel crowed and she turned lazy eyes to the clock. Seven. Dane began to mutter into her skin, his lips moving in tantalising sweetness. Then his whole body grew rigid and he moved away from her warily, leaving Jade with a terrible emptiness.

For a moment he hovered above her, his face still a little confused and drowsy, his shirt half unbuttoned so that Jade only had to reach her hand a little way to touch the crisp hairs on his chest.

'God!' he rolled from the bed and sat on the edge, his head in his hands. 'Sorry. I must have dozed off.'

'You're very tired,' she said hoarsely.

He rose and stretched his limbs. 'I'm getting old. Anything you want from your house?' he asked lightly.

'Dane, I feel awful——'

'I know,' he said gently. 'It must be foul. Talking of fowl, I really must sort out those hens of yours. I'll bring breakfast in a little while.'

She lay in frustration, wishing her brain and her mouth would obey her and move a bit faster. She'd wanted to apologise properly and thank him properly. She wanted to end the feud between them and see where that led them both. Then she paused. Dane was intelligent enough to have known from her tone that she wasn't complaining about her own condition. He had deliberately chosen to misunderstand what she'd said to avoid any heart to heart with her.

For some reason he wanted to keep their relationship on a casual, light footing. And the only reason she could think of was that he wanted to be shot of her as soon as possible, and not get involved again.

*   *   *

After a few days she began to improve. Mrs Love still hadn't returned; Billy had been quite ill and Dane visited her again and blithely assured her that everything was going along fine at the manor.

The minute that Jade found herself responding too eagerly to Dane's unwittingly sensual bed-baths, she stopped him and said she would manage in future. He seemed relieved not to have the chore any longer, though it took her a long time to wash herself, and the whole process left her exhausted.

He'd bring her up some tea and thin bread and butter afterwards, and this time he'd added strawberries to coax her appetite.

'Try some,' he urged. 'You need to eat. I can hardly find you on the bed when I come in nowadays.'

She smiled and tried a few of the ripe berries, knowing that she must get on her feet soon.

'I'm so awfully sorry,' she said weakly.

'What? What for?' he asked in surprise.

'For being such a nuisance.'

There was a silence. 'You're a nuisance when you're well, Jade Kendall, not when you're ill,' he said wryly.

She grinned. 'Swine,' she said gently.

'It's nice to see your dimple again,' he sighed. 'I thought it had been mumped away.'

That set Jade giggling till she felt weak. 'You've been very kind,' she said serious again. 'And it's taken a toll. Have you looked in the mirror lately?'

'I seem to remember something rather horrific staring back at me when I was shaving this morning,' he smiled.

'You look terrible.'

'I am terrible,' he said, snarling at her in fun.

'Be serious! I'm trying to say——'

'I know,' he said quietly. 'But I had treated you badly. I think I owed you.'

'Dane——'

'I think you'd better have words with your glands and tell them to subside,' he said briskly. 'Try to get better fast. Your bees look a bit gloomy. I haven't had time for a chat with them lately. I thought of shoving them on the bar at the Vine each evening, to partake of the local gossip, but the landlord said he didn't allow under-age bees in his pub.'

'You're mad,' smiled Jade, realising he still didn't want to get bogged down in sensitive discussions. 'How have you coped with the hens?'

'No trouble. My father had a few thousand, so your lot don't trouble me much.'

'Oh, yes,' she said, 'he had a farm. Tell me about your family.'

'Not much to say. I told you they're in the Algarve. They sold up their farm and took early retirement. We've always been close. Soniver and I are, too. Despite our appearances, we feel more at home in the country. So I'm not a City man at heart,' he said, gently chiding.

'No,' she said. 'I don't think you are. Dane . . . can I ask you a personal question?'

'Depends.' He seemed to be holding his breath.

'What happened for your marriage to break up?' Jade was wondering if he'd been unfaithful. If he had . . . she must draw back into her shell.

He went over to the window and stood there, looking out for a long while, before coming back to sit on the bed and hold Jade's hand, staring down at it.

'She was pregnant. I was delighted. We hadn't planned on children at that stage, because she was a dancer and had just landed a fantastic part in a Broadway musical. To be honest, we didn't see each other that often with all our commitments. Anyway, the pregnancy was an accident and she was furious. The next thing I knew was that she'd had an abortion.' Jade anguished with him, putting up with the bruising grip that was crushing her hand. 'Things went rapidly downhill after that,' he continued in a low voice. 'It was all over the moment she killed our child. Somehow I couldn't bring myself to want her after that. The body is a strange mechanism.'

'Yes, it is,' she said softly.

That evening, Dane didn't sit with her as usual. He made an excuse, saying he had to work. She saw little of him over the next few days as she was getting on her feet, and the hours were emptier because of that. His tender concern for her and his uncomplaining hard work had swayed her judgement of him. No man could be that selfless and be a prize bastard. And his confidences about his ex-wife had touched a chord in her heart. He wasn't only concerned with building a business empire, he wanted children too, and had been devastated when his wife had denied him their child, judging by his choking voice.

Her resistance to him was on increasingly weak ground—yet their physical relationship was over. Like the purple trumpet of the Morning Glory flower, it had been short-lived: blossoming with exuberance and then fading. He disliked her. Perhaps hated her. Only his huge capacity for helping anyone who was weaker, vulnerable, or in need of comfort, had made him look after her. But, as he had said, when she was completely well again she would be her usual thorn in his side.

She had slept during the late afternoon, bored and lonely, and couldn't settle that night. Feeling restless and tired of being cooped up in the bedroom, she quietly drew on her long, flowing kimono, which her parents had once bought her. The pale blue silk felt cool on her naked body as she fastened it with its wide sash. She tiptoed downstairs to the conservatory, knowing it would be warm from the day's sun. The tiles made her bare feet icy, though, and she slipped into a big basket chair, curling up in it like a lithe cat. The robe fell open and she saw how thin her thighs were. Frowning, she opened the top of the kimono a little, afraid that her breasts had suffered.

'God, Jade!'

She gave a little scream and clutched at the sides of the chair.

'Sorry.' Dane was half hidden under the Stephanotis, whose strong scent pervaded the whole room.

'You startled me,' she breathed, mesmerised by his hypnotically sensual eyes.

'You sure as hell startled me,' he muttered, raking her body avidly.

'I couldn't sleep,' she explained in a croak.

'Really?'

His tone was disbelieving. 'It's true,' she protested.

'So you walked down here, chose the exact same place as I did by accident, arranged yourself seductively in the chair and began to bare your breasts!' he said savagely.

With an angry gesture, he reached for a bottle and poured himself a stiff drink. Whisky, thought Jade. He's been drinking.

'Didn't you come down to seduce me?' he asked.

'No! I didn't know you were here,' she said, covering herself up quickly. 'I—I when I sat down, I happened to notice how much weight I'd lost. That's why I . . . looked.' It sounded unlikely, even to her ears.

'Afraid you'd lost your sexy curves?' he sneered.

'I don't want to talk to you while you're like this,' she said, rising.

His arm snaked out and caught her wrist. Jade didn't

struggle, she knew she was too weak, and he was inflamed with some kind of angry passion and the whisky. She stood, as cold as an iceberg.

'Frigid again. I burn for you and you go tight. Why can't you feel the same way about me as you did about your late husband?' he growled.

'Dane! Don't!' she moaned. 'Let's not talk about it.'

'I want to,' he said, pulling her on to his knee. 'I want you to tell me about him.'

'No!'

His fingers were running up the silk, tracing the line of each breast, and she was powerless to stop him. Then he opened the front of the kimono and his hungry mouth fastened on her breast, feasting. Jade's eyes closed and her hands came up to cradle his head.

Then he was covering her up again and pushing her off his lap as if he despised her. She felt as if she'd been slapped violently in the face. Every part of her body was crying out for him; with a few swift and expert moves, he had reduced her defences to nothing. But he was well able to stop, even when he'd had a couple of glasses of whisky to loosen his inhibitions.

'I hate you!' she cried, half believing it. 'I *hate* you!'

Her dash upstairs to the bedroom went unchecked. She didn't even need to have locked the door. Dane didn't bother her. In the morning he had gone, leaving a note to say that she could stay till she felt better, but he would be in London for a while and she'd have to ask Charlie to feed the animals.

Weak and vulnerable, her head aching from trying to work out why she still persisted in wanting and loving Dane, Jade lay gloomily on the bed for hours. It seemed they had both closed the door on one another with a terrifying finality.

CHAPTER TEN

THE tiny church of Saxonbury was packed for the Harvest Festival. Tier upon tier of fruit, vegetables and flowers had been arranged in every available space, and the air was filled with the smell of the produce. Mrs Love laid her masterpiece in the centre of the display before the altar. It was a massive golden wheatsheaf, baked in crusty bread.

There was a space next to Jade, who wiggled along a little to make room for Mrs Love's broad hips.

'Mr King's back,' she whispered. 'So he will read the Lesson, after all.'

Jade gave a weak smile, waiting for Dane to come by and take up his position in the manor pew which was opposite the choir stalls and ran at an angle to the congregation's pews. When he arrived, she couldn't prevent herself from staring wistfully, absorbing everything about him.

He looked unwell, but it suited him in an odd kind of way. He wore one of his impeccably tailored suits: charcoal-grey with a gossamer-fine white stripe, hugging his wide shoulders and deep chest and flaring subtly at the double vents. His shirt, a blinding white, showed deep cuffs at the wrists and large gold cuff-links, which picked up the colours of his favourite gold tie and handkerchief.

His long fingers flicked over the pages of his hymn book as he searched for the first hymn. Jade was riveted by his expression. His sky-blue eyes had lifted to the pillar above the lectern, where a board announced the numbers, and she had been shocked at how dead his eyes looked, as if nothing was behind them: no emotion, no feeling, no life. And his face was thinner than she remembered and less bronzed, the bones of his cheeks gleaming in the guttering candlelight which lit his pew and which cast deep shadows in the hollows of his face.

They rose to sing. His dark head bent, his dark brows frowned. It seemed that he was only murmuring the words. As the joyous notes rang out, sung with enormous gusto by the packed congregation, he seemed to falter and then stopped singing altogether.

A lump filled Jade's throat and she, too, was unable to continue.

'All right, dear?' asked Mrs Love.

Jade nodded, pointing to her throat as though she was still having trouble from the after-effects of mumps. The ordeal was over. She could sit down and let her trembling legs recover.

Dane put down his book and strode to the pulpit and began to read the Lesson. His deep, velvety voice rang out strongly, capturing everyone with its passion and sincerity. Jade wanted to cry. He looked so heartwrenchingly lonely up there, distant and withdrawn, and yet she knew him so well. She admired him more than anyone she had ever known and she would love him all her life.

To hold back the tears, she turned her gaze away towards the narrow Norman window at one side and watched the pigeons flying down to feed on the stubble. The rest of the service continued and Jade had never felt the intensity of life so much before as she stood in that little church, with Dane so near and yet so far. The final hymn rose to the rafters as the villagers sang exuberantly and the organist pulled all the stops out on the organ to swell the church with sound.

Blurred by tears, Jade kept her head down and slipped past Mrs Love and through the small side door, unwilling to become involved in the invitations which would be generously given by villagers who continued the celebration with harvest suppers. She wanted to be alone. To hell with her tidy saffron silk dress, she'd climb the oak tree and let the beauty of the early autumn evening drift over her and calm her jangled nerves.

'*Jade.*'

Her hand flew to her breast in despair. Not now, not while she felt so vulnerable! She pretended not to hear and walked on, climbing the stile and walking along the footpath to the oaks with rapid steps. He was following her. She reached the tree and touched its rough bark with desperate fingers, knowing that he was bearing down on her. As his footsteps neared, she whirled around, flattening herself defensively against the tree.

Her black hair feathered out in the breeze, which caught the bright saffron skirt and lifted it gently around her tanned legs. Her face was dark in the shadow of the tree, her eyes and teeth between her parted lips a glistening white.

'About your book, Jade,' he said, his face devoid of expression.

Her body sagged in relief. Then she smiled wryly. He hadn't greeted her properly, or observed the normal conventions usually followed by people who hadn't seen each other for a while. It appeared he wanted to come straight to the point so he could go.

'I'm not using the library any more,' she said, 'if that's what's worrying you. I've finished the book. It's being typed.'

'Who?'

She frowned, wondering what it had to do with him. 'An agency in Lewes.'

'Do you have an agent? Have you approached publishers? I never did ask whether you were writing on spec. or had already been commissioned on the strength of a couple of chapters.'

'You were never interested,' she said lightly. That had hurt a little.

'It seemed unwise for me to get involved professionally with you,' he said quietly.

'It was unwise to get involved unprofessionally,' she said, tipping up her chin.

'Answer the question,' he grated.

She was riled by his impatience to get away once he'd completed his business, whatever that was.

'I haven't approached anyone yet. This was such a far cry from anything I'd done before, I didn't know how long it would take and didn't want to be chained by some deadline.'

'I have an agent for you,' he said.

'Well——' She wasn't sure she wanted any favours.

'He's very good. Harriet says your book has an easy style that will make it popular with the general public—and the sketches are delightful. Naturally I don't want to handle it——'

'Naturally.'

He glared. 'This man will see that the book receives publicity and the maximum sales possible.'

'I'm not worried about the money,' she said slowly. 'I have enough to live on, but . . .'

'You'd like more people to know about their heritage, and for strangers to get more out of visits to the area,' he suggested.

Dane King was too perceptive by far! Jade regarded him doubtfully.

'I'm not sure.'

'You wouldn't lose anything by trying him. Here's his card—give him a ring and mention my name. Ask if he'd be willing to see the typescript. He may even refuse.'

Jade bristled as she took the card, at the idea of a refusal. It was her best work so far! Then she saw that Dane's eyes were gleaming. He'd said that on purpose! The man was a positively accomplished manipulator!

'Thank you,' she said, determined to send the book off to the man as soon as possible. She'd prove to Dane that her work was good enough to be accepted.

Hoping he'd go now, she waited by the oak. But he continued to look at her, an inscrutable expression on his face, and Jade began to feel uncomfortable.

'Well, if that's all,' she said, 'I want to be alone.'

Her tongue slicked over dry lips and his face became as black as thunder. Tightening her mouth, she turned and, disregarding him completely, kicked off her smart peep-toe shoes and reached up to the first branch. Before she could haul herself up, though, his hands had grasped her waist and she gasped at the way they encompassed it, making her feel intensely feminine as his warmth burned fiercely through the thin silk.

'I have to talk to you,' he said hoarsely.

She pulled away, to escape his bone-melting touch, and his hands slid over her hips as she moved upwards. Then he had let her go and, with trembling limbs, she made her way on and up, over the great branches and into the smooth fork, knowing that her dress had been ruined in the impulsive climb, but shakingly aware that it had been essential to get away from Dane.

She looked down on his upturned face, set in anger, and then lifted her head and fixed her eyes on the gentle beauty of the valley in all its autumn richness. The view was framed by the oak tree's branches, silhouetted against the pinkening sky of the sunset, the evening light shining right through the yellow, gold and brown leaves so their fine veins showed clearly. Jade relaxed.

Then she heard him coming up after her and realised she would be trapped. It made her feel furious that he wouldn't leave her alone, but had to hound her like this. What was he going to do? Twist the knife by telling her they must keep their distance, that he didn't want anything to do with her and he hoped she'd realise that?

His head appeared by her thigh, his eyes baleful.

'You've torn your dress,' he said.

'I don't care,' she answered sullenly. 'Can't you see I'll do anything to get away from you? You don't have to worry that I'll follow you down the lane and make sheep's eyes. I've got over my stupid passion. It must have been sex starvation, as you said.'

Her voice had become sharp and wounding as she became more desperate in her attempt to sever the ties between them. For all the time she spoke, she wanted to kiss his angry mouth, to slide her tongue between his lips which he had parted in a snarl, and her defence became fiercer.

'Jade,' he said in a harsh whisper, 'there is something unfinished between us, and I won't leave you alone until it has been cleared. There are things I have to know.'

'There's nothing you need to know about me,' she cried.

'Will you come down and talk to me, or do I have to put you over my shoulder and carry you down?' he rasped.

She stared at the grim face. There was no doubting his determination. Jade hoped she would be able to keep her dignity and pride during his cross-examination.

'If you swear to leave me alone afterwards, and not keep bothering me like this, I'll come down of my own accord and talk to you,' she said reluctantly.

'If that's what you want.'

His head disappeared and Jade climbed down, wishing her dress didn't keep riding up. On the lowest branch, she pulled her skirt down over her scratched thighs and poised to jump, relieved that he didn't offer to catch her. But when she landed on all fours like a cat, he was there, his hands on her waist, helping her up. She shook him off impatiently.

'Come and sit by the river,' he said, his mouth hard.

They went to the old landing-stage, where the huge stones had once been brought from France to build both the priory and the church, nine hundred years ago. Jade was carrying her shoes and sat, dangling her toes in the cold water. The sky was now a fiery red, casting an unearthly glow on Dane's face. She gulped as he came to sit beside her, and moved away a little.

'All right, you've made your point,' he muttered.

'What do you want to say?'

'Clarify,' he amended. 'It's because of Soniver. She says that until I get things straight, I won't settle to work. I have to get my past clear before I can make any kind of future for myself.'

Jade bit her lip at the thought that his future wouldn't include her in any way at all. But he was right: if they could get all their hostility laid out and in the open, it might help her to see how far apart they were in every way.

'Go on,' she said coolly.

'I want to know first why you sized me up the way you did. Virtually from the moment you saw me, you decided I was a prize bastard and yet you had no reason to think that. Why, Jade?'

'Intuition,' she mumbled.

'It's more than that. I think you gave yourself away when you declared I'd be holding wild parties and orgies at the manor, with nude bathing. It's something to do with Sebastian, isn't it? I know how painful it is, Jade, when I mention his name. It hurts me when I speak of my lost, unborn child,' he said, agony on his face. 'But it will help us both if we understand the reasons for our antagonism. Tell me. Trust me.'

His tone had become so gentle and concerned that her heart wrenched, both for him and for herself.

'You were like them,' she said, trying to find a way to tell him. 'Sebastian's friends. Smart, well-groomed, sophisticated. They were all living life in the fast lane: snazzy cars, elegant girlfriends. We had parties during which they virtually took the house apart.'

'And you didn't like that?' he asked quietly.

'No. To begin with I thought it was high spirits, but I soon realised it was a complete disregard for property and anyone's feelings,' she said.

'Didn't Sebastian try to control his guests? Or did he merely stop holding the parties?'

'He was in the thick of it all,' she said miserably.

'That must have been difficult, with both of you wanting different life-styles,' he said. 'I can understand how you didn't want the new owner of the manor to be a carbon copy of your late husband.'

'Oh, you're not a bit like him!' she cried passionately. 'For a start, you don't hold parties like that!'

'At least you recognise one difference,' he said, his mouth twisting. 'You're an exuberant person; why couldn't you enjoy the fun?'

'It was more than honest fun,' she said in a low voice. 'You see, Dane, I'd been brought up to honour my parents' values. At home I was surrounded by creative, deep-thinking people who appreciated the quality of life and fitted in with my mother's ideas about morality. She was sensual in the Italian way, but very proper.'

His eyes ran over her gently blowing hair and studied her brooding face. 'I see.'

'When they died, my life seemed to stop. I didn't know

what hit me. Sebastian and I had met at a concert—we liked the same music—and he'd been taking me to dinner and concerts. To be honest, I don't know it happened, but he looked after me during that period, handling everything. He was a stockbroker and had the kind of brain that could untangle my parents' complicated money problems.'

'You married,' he said quickly. 'And came to live at the manor.'

'Yes,' she said, relieved that he hadn't asked if she loved Sebastian. 'I'm afraid he spent money lavishly on entertainments. It wasn't long before I discovered that his friends didn't have the same kind of morals that I did. I'd find various unmarried couples making love in the oddest of places, in broad daylight, and it shocked me, particularly when they swapped partners. Sebastian said I was bourgeois, and I suppose, for all my Bohemian life, I was.'

'Not necessarily.' Dane's voice had no expression in it at all. 'Is that when the dining-room got damaged, during a party?'

'Yes,' she breathed. 'It was his farewell party before he left for the ballooning attempt. He was always doing reckless things, driving through the village with his eyes shut and getting someone else to tell him when to turn the wheel, that kind of thing.' She was conscious that Dane was frowning hard. 'That was a party to end all parties,' she said with a mirthless laugh. 'Everyone got drunk and sick.'

Her throat had tightened and she couldn't go on.

'What is it, Jade?' he asked, at the sight of her anguished face. His arm stole around her shoulders and he moved close, so that his body warmed hers as the sun dipped below the horizon and the sky flared a dark blood-red for a moment and then a solemn, funereal purple.

'Tell me,' he added gently. 'Tell me what the problem is. I'm not sure I understand how a sensitive girl like you could be so much in love with someone like Sebastian, as you describe him.'

'Love?' she said in a cold, hoarse whisper, unable to keep up the pretence any longer. '*I hated him.*'

She felt shock run through Dane and closed her eyes. He held her for a while, rocking her, and then his thumb tipped up her chin.

'Tell me.'

For the first time in her life, she wanted to talk about it. Whatever he thought of her, despite the fact that he wanted to clear the air so they could go their separate ways, she could trust him, she knew that.

'He was an inconsiderate lover,' she began in a barely audible tone. 'He took and never gave. I was naïve and innocent when he married me, full of romantic ideas about marriage. He was often drunk, and I hated sex because it was so crude. That made him angry. I'd been very quiet during that last weekend, escaping from his guests whenever I could and only turning up to meals for appearances' sake. Late on the Sunday night, I went up to bed and found a strange couple in it. I can't tell you what they were doing, but I never wanted to use the bed again. I felt defiled by it.'

'Hell! I'm going to get rid of the damn thing!' Dane's hands held her tightly, enabling her to go on.

'There were people in my studio, too. So I went into Sebastian's study and curled up on the couch. He came in, wanting to make love, and I just couldn't. He would have tried another woman, I suppose, but at that stage in the evening they were all occupied,' she said bitterly.

'Wait a minute. Are you telling me he was unfaithful? To you?' he asked in astonishment.

'Yes,' she said, ashamed. 'He said I was frigid and not much fun, and I began to believe him, believe there was something wrong with me. Every time I saw him kissing another woman at a party I'd grow even colder towards him. I didn't want him, Dane, you understand! You felt the same way towards your wife!' she cried, desperate for someone to understand her feelings.

'Jade, of course I know how you felt. Go on. He came to the studio and tried to make love to you. Is that why you cried out "not again, Sebastian" that time when we were together?'

'Yes.'

He gave a self-mocking laugh. 'I thought our lovemaking had reminded you of your husband, and you were so wrapped up in him that his was the first name that sprang to your lips. God, that hurt my pride!'

'I know. I'm sorry. I couldn't tell you then. You see, he said it was the last time he'd see me for a few weeks, and he was determined to . . . to . . .' She broke off, remembering, and struggled to control herself, knowing by Dane's silence that he was controlling anger. 'He forced me,' she said in a whisper. 'Again and again, until I was physically sick. Then he hit me repeatedly, humiliating me with the things he said about my lack of femininity.'

'The swine!' grated Dane, his body tensed in fury.

'That was the last I saw of him.'

'So the next thing you heard was that he was dead.'

'Yes. And this is the part that has haunted me, Dane. When I heard, when his two friends came to tell me, I was *glad!*'

'Jade.' Dane turned her towards him and she was drawn against his chest in a secure embrace.

'I felt so guilty, Dane,' she mumbled into his shirt. 'He was my husband and he was a human being, and all I could think of was that I was free! I couldn't believe how low I had sunk.'

'Not you,' he crooned. 'Sebastian. You'd stayed your own true self all the time. It was a natural reaction, Jade, under the circumstances.'

'I felt sorry for him, and grief that it had happened after,' she said. 'But I still was shocked at my initial reaction. I didn't like the kind of person I was. So I withdrew from everything for a while, to try and calm myself down.'

'Every time you spoke his name or spoke of death, a terrible pain came into your face,' he said gently. 'I thought you grieved for him and your lost love.'

'Everyone thought that. I let them, because it meant they left me alone out of respect. I was unable to talk of it: I swept it out of my mind as much as I could so that it would go away. Then I discovered he had arranged a second mortgage on the house and we didn't have any money. Selling Saxonbury was mixed blessing. I loved the house itself and the area, but hated the memories.'

'Poor Jade.'

Dane was stroking her hair, his fingers gently pushing their way through the thick tresses to massage her scalp. Jade felt the familiar love and need for him rise within her, and couldn't cope with that in her emotional exhaustion.

'Thank you,' she said, moving back, still within the circle of his arms. She searched his face and saw concern there. 'You have helped me to face up to what happened. It seems all so long ago now, so much in the past. I am grateful.'

'I'm glad to have made things easier for you,' he said huskily.

Jade was unable to bear being near him any longer. Her pulses were jumping erratically.

'Right,' she said briskly. 'I'd better go now. It's dark.'

'Yes, of course,' he said, releasing her. 'I'm honoured to be the first person you've told your story to. Don't expect miracles: you may find it difficult to come to terms with what happened. It was a bad patch in your life in the same way that mine was. But the pain goes eventually. Thank you for trusting me.'

'Who better?' she asked lightly. 'Who else should I tell but Dane King, the man who is so capable at handling women?'

'Please,' he growled. 'Don't——' He paused and cocked his head, putting a finger to Jade's lips when she made to speak

There was a rustling in the wood—a noise louder than any woodland animal would make.

Dane leaned over and put his lips to her ear. 'Wait here,' he whispered.

At first, she was left quivering at the warmth of his breath, and then realised what he was intending. Already he'd begun to walk stealthily down the landing-stage, as if he was going to investigate the sounds. He looked back as Jade got up, and stopped her with a glance.

She watched him disappear into the dark wood in an agony of suspense. If that was a poacher, then Dane was unarmed and in danger. She began to tremble uncontrollably. Lately there had been a number of reports on the television where poaching gangs had boldly threatened gamekeepers and landowners with sawn-off shotguns, or crossbows. And there were roe deer in the wood.

It seemed to Jade that ice ran through her veins. She stood rooted to the spot by fear for Dane, all her senses alerted to the sounds in the wood. And then there was a noise which jerked her out of her immobility: a gunshot!

'Dane!'

Jade ran at full speed into the wood, the brambles tearing her dress, the sticks and small stones on the path bruising her tender instep. As she went further in, branches caught in her hair and scratched her face, but she plunged blindly on towards the heavy crashing that was coming from the undergrowth ahead.

She stopped at the edge of a glade, the weak moon filtering its pale light through the gap in the canopy of trees. In a tableau, Dane stood holding a man in an armlock, a dead buck at their feet.

'Dane!' she wailed.

'I'm all right, Jade. Get back!' he suddenly shouted, as they both were alerted to the sound of someone rushing through the wood from the path that led to the road.

'No!' she cried, running forwards. 'You'll be hurt!'

'Jade,' he grated, 'it'll be his partner. Hide. Look after yourself.'

She picked up the poacher's shotgun. 'I'm not letting anyone hurt you,' she said fiercely, pointing it at the oncoming assailant.

'Oh, *Charlie*!' Incredibly relieved as the supposed partner turned out to be the startled blacksmith, she lowered the gun. 'Oh, my God!'

'What is it?' said Charlie and Dane together, at her horrified face.

She raised her head slowly. 'I—I was going to kill some-one, to save you,' she said hoarsely.

'I don't think so,' grinned Dane, his eyes suddenly alive with silvery light. 'Not with the safety catch on.'

'I heard the shot. What happened?' demanded Charlie, picking up the gun.

'I arrived too late. This swine had already killed the buck,' said Dane grimly.

'Well, you got him, that's one good thing,' commented Charlie. 'Are you going to take him to the manor and give the police a ring?'

Dane looked at Jade, whose wide eyes still registered utter

relief.

'No,' he said with a smile. 'I thought you might, Charlie.'

'Me? I didn't catch him. Why . . .' His slow gaze travelled from Dane to Jade, who were gazing into each other's eyes and completely oblivious of everything around them. Dane's hands were already relaxing their grip.

With a grin, Charlie shouldered the gun and spun the poacher around, out of Dane's hands, clamping an even more painful iron hand around the man's wrists and pushing him towards the buck.

'Pick it up,' he ordered.

The poacher struggled to heave the buck on to his shoulders, and sullenly began the walk back to the road. Charlie's eyes were filled with amusement. He turned his head and looked at the couple who hadn't moved.

'He could have died, you know,' he yelled at Jade. 'He could have been blasted by shot.'

That ought to get her moving. He saw her shudder, and then he continued after the poacher, leaving them to it.

'You could have been killed, Dane,' Jade moaned. Then, as the enormity of the danger overwhelmed her, she rushed towards him, flinging her arms about his neck and holding him tightly. 'If you'd died . . . If . . . Oh, Dane,' she mumbled incoherently. 'I love you, I love you, I couldn't . . . Oh, it was awful!'

She was violently thrust away, the full length of his arms as he held her shoulders in a bruising grip.

'*What*?' he insisted, his fingers digging in deeply.

She pressed her lips together, wishing she didn't act on impulse, wishing . . .

'You said you love me,' he said in a low tone.

'Did I?' she squeaked.

'Stupid girl,' he murmured affectionately, shaking his head

in exasperation.

'Thanks,' she snapped.

'For how long? How long have you love me?'

She tried to avoid his gaze, but he forced her to look at him and repeated the question with a menacing softness.

'I can't remember,' she said reluctantly. 'A long, long time.'

'You said you hated me.'

'I know! I did! I hated you because you made me love you!' she cried defiantly.

'Stupid girl.'

'Don't keep *saying* that! I know I'm stupid! No one in their right mind would love you!'

His mouth twitched. 'I distinctly remember being half conscious after connecting with Charlie's fist, and you telling him that you had no feelings for me.'

Her lashes fluttered and she blushed. 'I thought you were listening,' she defended. 'I didn't mean it. I wanted to convince myself as much as you.'

'Why? Why not be honest?'

'Because you were—or I thought you were—entertaining dozens of women every week. They were going in and out of the manor like yo-yos. I didn't want to love a man who thought so little of women. And don't forget, I turned up one day to find Dodo lounging around in a see-through négligé and you totally unconcerned,' she said, wondering if he would explain that. She'd never been sure about his relationship with Dodo. 'She said it had been one hell of a night and you said something about overcoming her. And she was ravenous.'

He sighed and gave her a gentle smile. 'I'm so glad you were jealous. I hoped you would be, that's why I didn't explain at the time. Dodo had come to stay because it seemed the only way to force her to finish a script she was late in delivering. I bullied her all night and made her keep on writing, overcoming her need for sleep with gallons of coffee and almost constant snacks.'

'Oh.'

He laughed and drew her into her arms. 'Jade, I fell in love with you the minute I saw you on the verge. From then on, I was constantly on the verge. Do you remember how we picked up coins on the road? It was the maddest, most enjoyable thing I'd done for years. You hit me right between the eyes.'

'I did?' she asked, amazed.

'You did,' he said solemnly. 'And in other places, too. It astonished me that I couldn't keep my hands off you. I must have seemed very fresh.'

She had got over the shock of his words and elation lit her face, making her dimple dance.

'You *were* fresh,' she said in a disapproving tone.

'Well, I didn't like the way you magnetised me. I was disgusted with my lack of decency too, that I seemed helpless to prevent myself intruding on your grief. I wanted you so much, it seemed all my principles were being thrown overboard. I love you, Jade. I love you so much that I can't bear the thought of living without you. When I went away, it was as if the sun had gone out of my life. There in the church, it seemed to shine again because you were near, but the awful thing was that it wasn't shining for me. Everything seemed black where I was. I had to speak to you then, it was the only way I could think of exorcising you.'

'Exorcising!' she breathed. 'You exorcised a ghost for me.'

'You will marry me, won't you? We can have wonderful arguments about naming our children.'

She smiled. 'Arguments? Me, argue with you?'

'Yes, please,' he murmured. 'Then I can spend long hours persuading you to my way of thinking.'

'No, Dane,' she said, shaking her head with a laugh. 'I will spend long hours persuading you.'

'Can't wait,' he said huskily.

'We'll need the children before we argue over their names,' she pointed out.

'Exactly,' he grinned. 'Time we got started.'

'Oh, Dane! It's been hell, pure hell!'

'Hmmm. What . . . kind of hell, Jade?'

'Cold,' she said. 'Ice-cold. When I saw you disappearing into the wood to catch that poacher, my blood froze over. That was my hell: that we'd come to terms with each other at last and you'd be hurt, maybe killed. My body was turned to ice. Hell froze.'

'I knew it would freeze over one day,' he said, his rich, deep tones husky with sensuality. 'Now you must uphold your vow and surrender.'

'Yes, Dane,' she said, as meekly as she could.

He laughed at her false tone, belied too by the blazing fire of passion in her eyes. She laughed with him as they stood under the oak and, as his mouth tenderly claimed hers, she thought of the couples who had met here over the last few centuries, and wondered how many generations of the King family would come to the oak to make a lovers' tryst in the centuries to come. And then the immediacy of the present caught up with her as she learnt with Dane how sweet it was to love, really love.

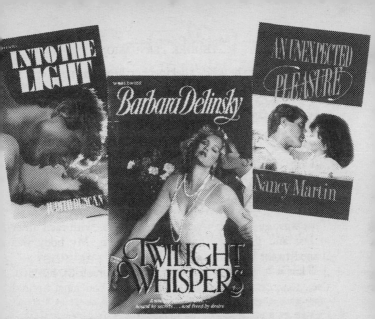

THREE TOP AUTHORS.
THREE TOP STORIES.

TWILIGHT WHISPERS — *Barbara Delinsky* — £3.50
Another superb novel from Barbara Delinsky, author of 'Within Reach' and 'Finger Prints.' This intense saga is the story of the beautiful Katia Morell, caught up in a whirlwind of power, tragedy, love and intrigue.

INTO THE LIGHT — *Judith Duncan* — £2.50
The seeds of passion sown long ago have borne bitter fruit for Natalie. Can Adam forget his resentment and forgive her for leaving, in this frank and compelling novel of emotional tension and turmoil.

AN UNEXPECTED PLEASURE — *Nancy Martin* — £2.25
A top journalist is captured by rebels in Central America and his colleague and lover follows him into the same trap. Reality blends with danger and romance in this dramatic new novel.

Available November 1988

W⦿RLDWIDE

Available from Boots, Martins, John Menzies, W.H. Smith,
Woolworths and other paperback stockists.

YOU'RE INVITED TO ACCEPT **FOUR ROMANCES** AND A TOTE BAG **FREE!**

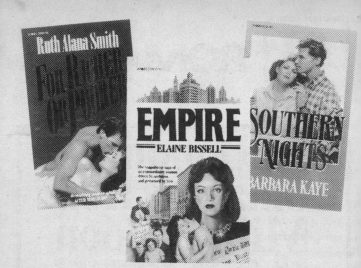

THE POWER, THE PASSION, AND THE PAIN.

EMPIRE – *Elaine Bissell* _____ £2.95
Sweeping from the 1920s to modern day, this is the unforgettable saga of Nan Mead. By building an empire of wealth and power she had triumphed in a man's world – yet to win the man she loves, she would sacrifice it all.

FOR RICHER OR POORER – *Ruth Alana Smith* _____ £2.50
Another compelling, witty novel by the best-selling author of 'After Midnight'. Dazzling socialite, Britt Hutton is drawn to wealthy oil tycoon, Clay Cole. Appearances, though, are not what they seem.

SOUTHERN NIGHTS – *Barbara Kaye* _____ £2.25
A tender romance of the Deep South, spanning the wider horizons of New York City. Shannon Parelli tragically loses her husband but when she finds a new lover, the path of true love does not run smooth.

These three new titles will be out in bookshops from December 1988.

W✪RLDWIDE

Available from Boots, Martins, John Menzies, WH Smith, Woolworths and other paperback stockists.